"Make excuses for yo... ...I know what happened that night was real."

Hardy kep... ...tting
lost in the... ...ed
to fight it,... ...ght.
What they... ...as
what he w...

He stepped close to her and cupped her face with his hands. Her skin was as smooth as anything he'd ever touched. He was always afraid to touch her, almost as if it was forbidden. He never understood why until this moment. Because she was the only woman who could make him lose himself. And he prided himself on control. Losing it for a second had brought on the guilt.

"It was real for me, too," he whispered against her lips.

Dear Reader,

In March of 2009 I published a book with the Harlequin American Romance line titled *The Sheriff of Horseshoe, Texas*. The story was about Wyatt Carson and Peyton Ross. In the book, Wyatt's best friend was Hardison (Hardy) Hollister and Peyton's friend was Angela (Angie) Wiznowski. I wanted to write Hardy and Angie's story, and I finally have. This is it: *One Night in Texas*.

So, we're going back to Horseshoe, a quaint little town in central Texas. Hardy is the DA and Angie's family owns the local bakery, which has been in Horseshoe through several generations of Wiznowskis. Angie is rooted in family and tradition and never plans to leave Horseshoe. Hardy has political aspirations and Horseshoe is only a stopgap to his future. They are two very different people with different goals in life. How was I going to bring them together and keep them together? It wasn't easy.

I had an idea for their story, but once I had it on paper I realized I had more story than I needed. Thus began the cutting process. Authors bleed and hurt when we have to do this. Really. It was painful. The good part, though, was I had a much better story. I hope you think so, too!

Until the next book, with love and thanks,

Linda Warren

You can email me at Lw1508@aol.com, or send me a message on Facebook, www.facebook.com/LindaWarrenAuthor, or Twitter, www.twitter.com/TexAuthor, or write me at P.O. Box 5182, Bryan, TX 77805. Visit my website at www.lindawarren.net. Your mail and thoughts are deeply appreciated.

ONE NIGHT IN TEXAS

—

LINDA WARREN

HARLEQUIN® AMERICAN ROMANCE®

Recycling programs
for this product may
not exist in your area.

ISBN-13: 978-0-373-75518-9

ONE NIGHT IN TEXAS

Printed in U.S.A.

ABOUT THE AUTHOR

Two-time Rita® Award-nominated and award-winning author Linda Warren loves her job, writing happily-ever-after books for Harlequin. Drawing upon her years of growing up on a farm/ranch in Texas, she writes about sexy heroes, feisty heroines and broken families with an emotional punch, all set against the backdrop of Texas. Her favorite pastime is sitting on her patio with her husband watching the wildlife, especially the injured ones that are coming in pairs these days: two Canada geese with broken wings, two does with broken legs and a bobcat ready to pounce on anything tasty. Learn more about Linda and her books at her website, www.lindawarren.net, or on Facebook, at www.facebook.com/AuthorLindaWarren.

Books by Linda Warren

ACKNOWLEDGMENTS

Special thanks to Britany Smith for her help and advice.
And, a big hug and thanks to Jaci and Addie Siegert
for answering my many questions. Love you girls.
And, thank you, Tammy Medina, for sharing about your
son's fractured femur. And, thanks to the ladies who
answered my questions about kolaches.

DEDICATION

To: Christi Hendricks and Carousel Paperbacks.
Thanks for fifteen years of fun book signings.

Chapter One

To Angela Wiznowski the sweetest sound in the world was her daughter's giggle: a bubbly gurgle erupting from her throat.

Angie leaned against the half-brick pillar on the porch of her bungalow-style house and watched Erin play in the front yard with her friends on a Slip 'N Slide. Today was her tenth birthday, and she'd had a fun-filled day. As the girls played with the water hose, shrieks and girlish laughter echoed through the late-May afternoon in Horseshoe, Texas.

Being a single mom hadn't been easy, but Angie must have done something right. Her daughter was happy. It was what Angie had done wrong that kept her awake at night.

The whole Wiznowski family had been there today, along with Angie's friends and neighbors. Everyone had come. Everyone except Erin's father.

Angie had made that decision a long time ago, but the remnants of guilt lingered. Maybe because it had been the wrong decision. A child had a right to know her father.

It was clear now. Back then, though, everything wasn't so black-and-white. It wasn't as if she hadn't tried to tell him, but he'd left town three days after they'd slept together for an extended vacation in Europe. Her attempts to contact him had failed. When he'd returned, he had an internship waiting for him in Houston. Angie had still tried to reach him, but when she found out he was engaged to someone else, she was devastated and unsure of what to do.

At eighteen, she'd felt alone and afraid. Keeping Erin's parentage a secret had never been a deliberate choice. It had just turned out that way. She couldn't tell him when he was set to marry another woman.

In college, Angie had met someone else, too, so fate had stepped in and the secret had stayed a secret. Part of her, the part that niggled at her late at night, knew Erin had missed a lot by not knowing her biological father.

Life went on, though. Her marriage had dissolved and she'd moved home to raise Erin alone. Although she wasn't alone, surrounded by her very large family in Horseshoe. Sometimes it just felt that way.

To make matters worse, two years ago Erin's father had returned to the small town and ran for the district attorney's office and won. He was now the D.A. Angie saw him almost every day. They had polite conversations like "How are you?" or "How's your family?" or "How are things at the bakery?" They were like strangers, as if that night had never happened. As if Erin had never happened.

Angie wrestled with her conscience daily, especially since his wife wasn't with him. Horseshoe was a small town and gossip was like a balloon—the more air blown into it, the bigger it became, and soon it was floating all over town with nothing to hold it up but a lot of hot air puffed up with half-truths.

Still, everyone listened to the gossip. It was better than boredom. The story was his marriage had ended years ago and he'd come home because his father's health was failing. She'd lost track of the number of times she'd marched to the courthouse to speak with him. He had a right to know, and she had to tell him even though her daughter might hate her.

But he was always in court or out of the office. She'd been waiting for the right time. When it came, he'd introduced her to his new girlfriend and she couldn't bring herself to tell him. Maybe she was just a coward. Fear kept her tied to her secret because she was afraid of losing what she loved most: her child. Erin's father was a lawyer and, even after all this time, he could try to take Erin from her.

Erin was starting to ask questions, too. One day Angie would have to tell her daughter about her father. Today was not the day. She dismissed the thought for now. The day of reckoning would come soon enough.

The afternoon was winding down and everyone had gone home except for two little girls and Jody, Erin's best friend, who were waiting to be picked up. The girls continued to play on the Slip 'N Slide, getting totally soaked, chasing each other with the hose.

Erin ran for the house. "Mama, I'm getting my beach ball. We want to play with it."

Angie started to stop her, but it was her birthday. They'd bought the ball at Walmart, getting ready for their summer vacation. They were driving to Disney World and stopping at every hotel/motel that had a pool until they reached the beach in Florida. Just Angie and her daughter. Erin would hit those teen years soon enough, and Angie wanted this special time with just the two of them.

Going to college and working, Angie depended on her family's support and help. Erin had three surrogate mothers in Angie's sisters. They adored their niece. At times, though, it was hard to have one-on-one time with her daughter. That was why Angie had moved out of her parent's home eight years ago and bought a house so she and Erin could have their own life.

The Polish-Catholic Wiznowskis were known for being a big family. Angie had four sisters and two brothers. Her brother Dale and her sister Dorothy had moved away right after high school. She was the youngest and often touted as the favorite, which was similar to being the little kid on the playground always picked on by the bullies.

Wyatt Carson, the sheriff, pulled up to the side of the house. His wife, Peyton, who was Angie's best friend, was with him. Peyton had gone home from the party so John Wyatt, otherwise known as J.W., their one-and-a-half-year-old son, could take a nap.

Wyatt came up the steps with his son in his arms. J.W. wiggled to get down and Wyatt let him. The baby scooted backward down the steps and tottered to his sister, Jody. He fell onto the Slip 'N Slide, laughing and getting soaked.

"Wyatt!" Peyton complained.

"He's a little boy. He wants to play."

Peyton wrapped her arm around her husband's waist. "You're changing him. I've done my quota for the day."

Wyatt kissed his wife. "The party over?" he asked Angie.

"Yes. Just waiting for two more parents."

Peyton was a beautiful blonde who was not the typical person you would find in Horseshoe. She had been raised in Austin in a wealthy family of social standing. She had made the mistake of speeding through Horseshoe one day, and Wyatt had arrested her because she'd had the nerve to try to bribe him. Who knew the sheriff and the socialite would fall in love? Peyton was now a small-town wife and mother. And happy. She and Angie had become fast friends through their daughters, and Angie treasured their friendship.

Two cars drove up to the curb. "The last of the birthday guests," Angie said. "It's been a long day."

The girls' squeals and giggles rose with excitement, and Angie glanced to where they were playing. They had the ball about twelve feet in the air, holding it there with the force of the water from the hose.

"Higher!" they shouted. Suddenly it bounced to the ground and toward the street. Erin ran after it.

"Erin, no!" Angie yelled.

Erin didn't hear her. Her concentration was on getting the ball back. Almost in slow motion Angie saw the truck coming around the corner. "Erin!" she screamed, but her daughter kept running in between cars to the street.

"No!" Angie sprinted down the steps and then froze in horror as she saw the truck slam into Erin, who flew up in the air and landed in a heap on the paved street.

In a matter of seconds Angie was at her child. Erin lay so still and pale. One of her legs was twisted in an unnatural way. A spot on her thigh was bruised and bleeding. Blood oozed into a dark red puddle. The sight sent fear burning through her.

Screams, shouts and sobs echoed through the perfect day and turned it into a nightmare. Someone kept screaming—a chilling sound. Angie wished they would stop. Her ears hurt from the loud noise, and then she realized it was her.

Wyatt knelt by her and put an arm around her. "Calm down."

Calm down. How did she calm down? Her child was lying like a limp doll in the street. Angie laid her face against Erin's warm one. Angie smelled bubble gum, and a sob caught in her throat. Her daughter loved gum.

Angie stroked Erin's wet hair and saw the bruise on her head and more blood. "Oh, my God!" She slipped a hand beneath Erin's head.

"Don't move her," Wyatt said. "An ambulance is on the way."

"Is…is she breathing?" They were the only words she could manage.

Wyatt laid his fingers against Erin's neck. "Yes."

Angie kept her face against her baby's. "Mama's here."

Through the bits and pieces of her control she heard a bird chirping. An inane thing when her child's blood was seeping onto the pavement. How could this happen? How could this day go from joy to horror?

"Angie, she came out of nowhere. I'm sorry."

She raised her eyes to the face of the man who had hit her child. Her heart jolted into a spasmodic rhythm and then just flatlined, leaving her struggling to breathe. Fate had stepped in with a fistful of vengeance. She stared into the deep blue eyes of Hardison Hollister.

Erin's father.

HARDY'S CHEST EXPANDED with raw terror. "I'm sorry, Angie. I didn't see her." His hands shook and his stomach roiled. He'd just hit an innocent child, and there was no way to make that better.

Angie glared at him with angry, unwavering eyes.

"It was an accident," Wyatt said. But it didn't change the sick feeling in his stomach as he stared at the little girl in the pink bathing suit with her leg twisted beneath her.

What was her name? He couldn't bring it up. Horseshoe was a small town, and everyone knew everyone. He and Angie had been more than friends once, but now they were mere acquaintances. They were civil to each other and often met by accident at Wyatt and Peyton's house. But he always kept his distance. Over the past two years, he'd been successful at that. How had he just hurt the one person she loved most in the world?

The blare of the siren whipped through the trees and roared to a stop not far from where they were kneeling on the pavement. Two paramedics jumped out with a stretcher. One began to ask questions. One was on the phone to the hospital, explaining the situation and checking the child's injuries. They quickly put a collar on the little girl and loaded her onto the stretcher and into the ambulance. A tearful Angie followed. Hardy's heart squeezed at the sight.

He glanced toward the house. Peyton held her son. Jody and two other girls were grouped around her, crying. Two women stood beside them. Someone needed to go with Angie. She didn't need to be alone. But everyone seemed frozen in shock.

He did the only thing he could. He climbed into the ambulance.

Angie eyes opened wide. "What are you doing?"

He sat on the side bench as the paramedics worked with the little girl to stop the bleeding. "Someone needs to go with you and since I caused all this, the logical person is me."

"There's no need," she said in a cool voice.

But there was no arguing. The ambulance zoomed toward Temple and the nearest hospital.

"How is she?" Hardy asked, not able to take his eyes off the child. She was so tiny. His chest grew even tighter as he saw blood soaking the stretcher.

"We've stopped the bleeding and started an IV," one paramedic answered. "Looks as if she's fractured her femur, but the doctors will give a better assessment once we reach the E.R."

Hardy stared at Angie and the years seem to roll back to a time they both wanted to forget. A time he had worked very hard to forget.

His sister, Rachel, and Angie were friends in high school. Their mother had been killed in a drive-by shooting while walking to her car at an Austin mall. She'd gotten caught in a fight between two gang members and was the only one to die. Her sudden death had hit the family hard. Rachel had been seventeen and crushed, as they all had been, but she couldn't seem to cope. Not until Angie had become a steadying force in her life.

Angie was sweet, kind, warm and giving. With her sunny disposition, she seemed to bring joy into a room. She had a sweet innocence about her that screamed "untouchable." Besides, she was his sister's age and too young for him.

Rachel had seemed to need Angie, and Angie had always been at the house. If she wasn't, Rachel was on the phone begging her to come. Angie had worked in the family bakery in Horseshoe, but she spent as much time with Rachel as she could.

Busy finishing up law school at the University of Texas, Hardy had rarely come home on weekends. But after his mother's death he'd come home often. Sometimes he had to wonder, though, if it was for his family or to see Angie. There was just something about her that made other people feel better—made him feel better.

Rachel had never liked to get dirty or sweaty. When they swam in the pool, Rachel would sit in a lounger while he and Angie frolicked in the water. He'd taught her to dive and how to hold her breath and open her eyes under the water. She'd been afraid to do that at first, and he'd laughed at her silly face when she finally did it. And he'd laughed when she'd made a belly buster off the diving board. He'd enjoyed being with her as much as Rachel did. Being six years older, sometimes he'd been ashamed to admit that.

Angie was a good cook and he lost track of the number of times she'd cooked in their kitchen—nachos, pizzas or anything Rachel wanted to eat. He'd eaten right along with them, soaking up the smile on Angie's face. They'd fought over movies. She had liked chick flicks, and he had liked action films. They'd done a lot of compromising and teasing. Rachel had been an artist and always drawing in her sketchbook and frowning at them. At times it had felt as if it were just the two of them in the world. He couldn't wait for Friday afternoons when he would head home to Horseshoe and Angie would be there.

God, that was so long ago. How could those memories still be so vivid? He took a long breath.

The sirens kept blaring as the ambulance sped toward Temple. It whipped in and out of traffic and zoomed through red lights. Other vehicles slowed and gave the ambulance right of way.

Oh, damn. He'd forgotten. He had a dinner date with his dad and Olivia in Austin. That was where he'd been going when he'd hit the little girl. He fished out his phone from his jeans and texted his dad and Olivia. Can't make it. Sorry. Been involved in an accident. I'm fine. I'll call later.

Messages immediately came back, wanting answers. Olivia and his dad were not very patient. He'd been dating Olivia on and off for about a year now. She understood him better than any woman he'd ever dated. But sometimes... He turned off his phone, not in the mood to answer questions. As he slipped the phone into his pocket, his eyes caught Angie's and his heart did a nervous hiccup.

Angie held her daughter's hand and stared at him with that incredibly hurt look he'd seen before. He looked away and let his thoughts drift.

Rachel had planned to study art in Paris. It was her first love. To help Rachel settle in, Hardison Sr. had decided they would take a family vacation to Europe. They'd been worried about Rachel being so far from home and her friends, especially away from Angie. Hardy had even thought of asking Angie to go with her friend, but he knew her morally upright mother wouldn't allow it.

Their father had thrown Rachel a big going-away party in August at the Hollister's ranch. Angie had been there. It was a party for teenagers, and he hadn't planned on making an appearance.

The party was supposed to end at twelve. He'd arrived home about twelve-thirty to find drunk teens around the pool. Someone had spiked the punch. His dad had been in bed, trying not to interfere with Rachel's fun. Hardy had called parents to come pick up their kids. His sister had been asleep on the sofa in the house, seemingly detached from her friends.

Going to his room, he'd found Angie in the hallway, sitting on the floor with her head on her knees.

"Are you okay?" he had asked.

"I feel woozy."

"Someone spiked the punch."

"I thought it tasted funny." She'd raised her head and rested it against the wall. "Everything looks unfocused."

"Come on. I'll take you home."

She'd gotten to her feet without a problem, but then she'd sagged against him. "I can't go home. My mama will have a fit. I don't do things like this and…"

He had helped her into his room. "Call your mom and tell her you're spending the night." Her mother, Doris, was known to be vocal and opinionated, and she would put Angie through the ringer. This wasn't Angie's fault. He hadn't seen the need to punish her.

Afterward, she'd stretched out on the bed and gone to sleep. He had started to wake her and tell her to go to Rachel's room, but she was sleeping so peacefully. After grabbing his toothbrush, he'd gone to a guest bedroom.

Sometime toward morning, he'd awakened and decided to check on her. Since she wasn't used to liquor, he was worried.

She had been sitting on the edge of the bed.

"Are you sick?" he'd asked from the doorway.

"No. I just feel like a fool."

He'd sat beside her in nothing but his pajama bottoms. He had realized later that he shouldn't have done that. "Most kids have tasted liquor before their eighteenth birthday, so consider it a rite of passage. You're now an adult."

She'd brushed her sandy-brown hair back from her face and smiled at him. Even with the room in semi-darkness, her smile was contagious. "Do you see me as an adult?"

"You're my sister's friend." He hadn't been sure how else to answer the question.

"That's it?"

"Angie…"

Before he could stop her, she'd reached over and kissed his cheek. He had breathed in the scent of her and should have pulled away. But he hadn't. She'd gently placed her lips on his and he was lost. He had wanted her in the worst way. He had wanted her the whole summer. Ignoring all the voices in his head, he'd kissed her back.

What had happened next was forever imprinted on his mind and on his heart. He'd taken her innocence.

There was no redemption for that.

Chapter Two

The ambulance wheeled into the emergency area of the hospital, and Erin was whisked inside. Angie climbed out without a glance at Hardy. She left him standing outside in the warm evening air. Pushing him to the back of her mind, she followed the stretcher.

She waited to the side as they examined Erin, her stomach a tangled mass of jittery nerves. Her baby looked so pale on the E.R. table. A nurse slit the new bathing suit with a pair of scissors and removed it. The doctor did a quick examination, calling out orders for tests that went over Angie's head. Her eyes were focused on her unconscious baby.

An X-ray had been done quickly, and the doctor put it up on a screen. "She has a fractured femur, a possible concussion and we have to check for internal bleeding and rib fractures. Let's get her up to the surgical ward. Notify Dr. Lawson and Dr. Robbins. Now." The man in the blue scrubs turned to Angie. "Are you the mother?"

Angie had to swallow twice before she could answer. "Yes."

"We're taking her for tests and then to surgery. Her left leg is badly fractured and will require surgery. The surgeon will talk to you before he operates. You'll have to sign papers."

"I need to be with her. She'll want her mama when she wakes up."

The doctor gave her a compassionate look. "I understand that, but she's not going to be awake for a long time." The doctor looked over her shoulder and asked, "Are you the father?"

Angie swung around to see Hardy standing there. Her pulse pounded in her ears as panic gripped her. She couldn't handle this now. Before words could leave her throat, Hardy stepped forward.

"I'm Hardy Hollister. The girl ran out in front of my truck and I hit her. Please do whatever you can to help her."

"We will."

Two nurses came in and pushed Erin's bed toward the elevator. Angie was one step behind. She didn't know why Hardy was still there. She wanted him to leave.

A nurse pointed to a door. "You can wait in there. After the tests, the surgeon will talk to you."

"Thank you." She took a deep breath and walked inside feeling empty, alone and scared out of her mind. Her baby had to be okay.

Without even having to look, she knew Hardy was behind her. His presence was strong and undeniable. But she was strong, too. He'd made her that way.

She faced him. "Would you please leave?"

"I have to know that she's okay."

"Wyatt will call you."

He shook his head. "I'm not leaving, Angie. You don't need to be here alone."

Alone? Is he kidding?

"My family is on the way. You're just a stranger to me, and I don't want you here."

His tanned skin paled. "I'm not a stranger." Her words

might have stung, but being an attorney he was used to brushing away barbs as no more than pesky flies. Just like he did women.

As a teenager, Angie had been so naive and in love with the fantasy of Hardison Hollister: tall, handsome, older and a little mysterious. She used to dream about her friend's brother. It had to be love, because she thought about him all the time.

Suffering through the remnants of a hangover, she'd gained the courage to show him she was an adult. To maintain her sanity, she'd closed her mind to what had happened next.

It was a mistake, he'd said. He was sorry, but she was his sister's friend and she could never be anything else to him. So she'd taken her mangled pride and did the best she could with a broken heart. Even now when she saw him around town or with one of his many women, she'd have the oddest moments where she thought she still had those feelings for him. Maybe some fantasies never died.

But she was older, mature and Hardy wasn't going to mess with her mind again. She wanted him to leave so she could deal with her injured child. Later, she'd have to divulge her innermost secret. Not now, though.

She looked him straight in the eye. "It was an accident. I don't hold you responsible. Is that what you're waiting to hear?"

His eyebrows knotted together. "No. I'm genuinely concerned for her."

"Really? What's her name?"

"Uh…what?"

"You've avoided me for two years. Let's don't change things now."

"You look at me as if I'm a leper or something. I can't go back and change the past, but I'm not leaving this hospital until I know your daughter is out of surgery and doing well."

"I don't want you here. Can't you understand that?" Her control slipped a notch.

His question, "Why?" blasted through her control with the force of a bullet, and it pierced through regions of her heart she'd kept safe. Safe from any emotions she might have had for him. Safe from admitting she was just as gullible as she'd ever been.

TWO DOCTORS IN scrubs and surgical caps walked into the room, preventing Angie from answering. Not that she had an answer she could share with him. She immediately went to the doctors.

One looked down at the chart in his hand. "Ms. Wiznowski?"

"Yes."

"I'm Dr. Lawson, and this is Dr. Robbins, a pediatric orthopedist."

They shook hands. "How's my daughter?"

Dr. Lawson looked over her shoulder, and Angie cringed. She knew what the doctor would ask next.

"Are you the father?" he asked Hardy.

Hardy stepped forward. "No. I hit her with my truck. She came out of nowhere."

The doctor nodded. "It's commendable you're taking responsibility."

"How is my daughter?" Angie didn't know why the doctor was talking to Hardy. Erin was no concern of his. That wasn't quite true, but she couldn't admit that now.

Dr. Lawson turned his attention to her. "Your daughter has taken quite a beating, but she's young and has no life-threatening wounds."

Angie sagged with relief. "Thank God."

"But we do have some concerns. She has a bad cut on her head from hitting the pavement. We've used surgical tape to close it. She has two fractured ribs, but no internal bleeding. Our main concern is her leg. Dr. Robbins will discuss that with you. I just wanted to let you know she's resting comfortably."

"Thank you. Can I see her?"

"My surgical team is prepping her for surgery," Dr. Robbins answered. "We need your permission to continue. The nurse will bring some papers in for you to sign."

"Okay. Her femur is broken?" she asked.

"Yes. Severely, but I can operate and repair it. I'll insert a lightweight titanium rod to stabilize the fracture." He opened the file and drew as he talked. "It's a new technique. I'll make an incision on the top of her hip. Right about here." He made a mark on the stick figure he'd drawn. "After I realign the bone, I'll insert the rod through the center of the bone, which will then serve as an internal splint."

"Will she need a cast?"

"No. We might put an immobilizer on her knee at first to prevent movement. These fractures take about six weeks to heal. In the meantime she'll be on crutches so she can keep her weight off that leg. In a year, we'll remove the rod."

"So the prognosis is good?"

Dr. Robbins nodded. "Yes. I deal with a lot of femur fractures, and they heal beautifully, especially in young children. It just takes time."

Angie thought of the wonderful vacation they'd planned and how excited Erin was to see Disney World. Now they would be spending the summer at home, healing and trying to come to grips with what had happened.

"Can I see her, please?"

"She's in a sterile area. You won't be able to see her until after surgery."

"If she wakes up and I'm not there, she'll be so afraid."

Dr. Robbins touched her shoulder in a reassuring gesture. "I promise you, you'll be there when she wakes up."

"Thank you. How long will this take?"

"Maybe an hour or so, depends how everything goes. I'll come back and talk to you when it's over."

The doctors walked out, and she felt more alone than ever. But Erin was going to be okay.

She took a deep breath and turned to deal with Hardy. "Erin is going to be okay. You don't need to feel guilty anymore."

"I know your ex-husband isn't part of your life anymore, but shouldn't he be notified?" he asked as if it was his right to do so.

"That's none of your business."

"No matter what your relationship is, he has a right to know his child has been injured."

She hated it when he took on his lawyer persona and kept probing until he got the answers he wanted. But he would be the last person she would tell about Dennis Green, her married-in-haste ex-husband.

"I'll take care of it."

"I'd like to try to explain. I need to explain."

She also hated that honorable streak in him. Before he'd left for Europe, she'd seen him in town and they'd sat on a bench at the courthouse and talked for a few minutes. He had apologized once again for what had happened and wanted her to know how much he liked her and he wished her all the best in the future. Being young and incredibly naive, she'd wanted words of love and marriage.

When she'd found out she was pregnant, her first thought had been she had to tell him. But Hardy had been in Europe, and she'd had no way to get in touch with him. She'd kept praying Rachel would call and then she could talk to Hardy, but the call never came.

She had agonized over how to tell her mother—her very strict, religious mother. Patsy and Peggy, her twin sisters, were in Temple going to beauty school. She'd joined them there to attend Temple Junior College and take accounting courses. It had been her way to escape a confrontation with her mother and to escape the gossip, if only temporarily. Still, she couldn't sleep or eat. She'd been a mess. Then she'd met sweet and kind Dennis, and her world had righted itself.

A nurse entered the room with some papers and a clipboard in her hand. She looked at Hardy. "Mr. Wiznowski?"

Angie wanted to scream with frustration. Why did they think Hardy had anything to do with Erin? *Because he does. He is her father.* He just didn't know it.

The truth of that opened the blinds she'd firmly kept shut against such observations. Eighteen-year-old Angie had thought she could save her pride and spare her feelings from being shattered by walking away and raising her child alone. That had been foolish. Twenty-eight-year-old Angie could clearly see that. The blinds were wide-open and the outside world was creeping in slowly but surely. Her day of reckoning had arrived.

She had been six weeks pregnant when she'd heard that Judge Hollister, Hardy's father, was back from Europe. He had been a judge in the small town for almost forty years. The thought of Hardy not knowing had bothered her, so she'd gone home early one Friday to talk to the judge in hopes that she could get Hardy's number. Instead, he'd thought she wanted to talk to Rachel and made the call so they could visit. Looking back, she should've asked Rachel for the number. But Rachel had gone on and on about Paris, and the moment had slipped away.

Fear and guilt had kept her steady company. To ease her mind, she'd made the trip again. As before, the judge had thought she wanted to speak to Rachel and made the call. Rachel hadn't answered, and it gave Angie a chance to ask the judge how Hardy was doing.

That was when she'd learned that he was engaged and planning a Christmas wedding. The man had been thrilled that Hardy had met the perfect woman for him. She would be an asset to his burgeoning political career.

Angie had been devastated, and Dennis had been there to console her. When he'd offered to marry her, she'd accepted. It had been a way out. She wouldn't have to face her mother or the gossip. How weak she'd been. Goose bumps popped up on her arms and a chill ran through her. She'd made so many mistakes. The burden of them would always be with her.

Lost within herself, she hadn't even noticed a nurse was talking to Hardy. That was typical. Women were drawn to him.

She cleared her throat. "Do you have papers for me to sign?"

"Oh." The nurse thrust the clipboard at her. "Read and sign at all of the marked x's."

Angie sat in one of the chairs, read and signed the papers, very aware that Hardy was watching her.

Handing the clipboard back, she asked, "Do you know if they've started the surgery?"

The nurse shook her head. "I just deal with the paperwork."

"Thank you."

The nurse looked at Hardy, then walked out.

It wasn't the time to shatter his world, and Angie didn't know if she had the strength to tell him now. Or in the future. She had to keep her focus on Erin. But later, when Erin was better, she would pull the Band-Aid off her heart and open it up to whatever came next.

Just like years ago, it would take all the courage she had, even take a part of her stubborn pride, but it had to be done. Hardy had missed ten years of Erin's life, and he would never forgive her for that. Somewhere in that maze of emotions, though, they had to find a way to get along—for their child.

Hardy eased into the chair next to her. A light, musky scent reached her, and she resisted the urge to move away. In jeans, boots and a pristine white shirt, he was as handsome as ever. In the old days, looking at his long legs and broad shoulders would send her heart soaring to the heavens faster than the speed of light. Now her heart was numb. Maybe because she was looking at him through the eyes of her conscience.

"I was talking to the nurse about Dr. Robbins. She said he's a very good pediatric orthopedic surgeon, so you don't have anything to worry about. Your daughter's going to be fine. Maybe a little bruised, but fine."

She looked into the dark blue eyes of the man she had loved deeply, or thought she had. Oddly, today she only saw a man she'd hurt. She swallowed. "Her name is Erin."

"What? Oh. That's pretty."

God, she couldn't believe he didn't know Erin's name. Suddenly ten years of keeping a secret felt like a boulder on her chest. How did she make this right? Could she make it right? There had to be an answer somewhere.

"I'll pay for anything she needs," he offered.

"I have good insurance." She started to say it wasn't

any of his concern, and she began to think that maybe she was the one who'd received the bump on the head. Unexpectedly, she saw herself as a woman she didn't like. A woman who kept secrets. A woman who'd lied.

Bile rose up in her throat.

"Are you okay?" He reached out to touch her and she jerked back.

"Don't touch me." If his skin touched hers, she would lose what little self-respect she still maintained. The memory of his skin against hers was still vivid after all these years. The warmth, the passion, would always be part of her because they'd created Erin. She could not remain strong when he was gentle and understanding.

Footfalls pounded against the tiled floor and the door flew open. The Wiznowski family charged in. The whole group grabbed her in a hug. Her legs buckled. The support of her family held her upright.

Over her sister's shoulder she saw Hardy moving toward the door. Her mother noticed it, too.

"How could you hit our precious Erin? Were you drinking or on your phone?"

"No, ma'am."

"Why weren't you paying attention, then?"

"I was. She just came out of nowhere," Hardy replied stiffly.

"She's just a little girl." Tears filled Doris's eyes, and Angie hugged her mother.

"It was an accident, Mama. The doctor said Erin's going to be okay. She just needs surgery on her leg and time to heal."

"Thank God."

"Is she in surgery?" Patsy asked.

"Yes."

"So we wait." Patsy sank into a chair, as did Peggy,

AnaMarie, her other sister, and their dad, Willard. Doris kept staring at Hardy. Angie just wanted some peace and quiet and not to have to referee family squabbles.

Her brother Bubba entered the room, and, before anyone could stop him, he swung his right fist at Hardy, who staggered backward from the blow to his jaw. He didn't go down, which was a feat, because Bubba was six foot two and weighed about three hundred pounds.

"Stop it," she said, getting between the two men.

"He hurt Cupcake." Bubba raised his fist again. "I'm gonna kill him."

"Cupcake ran out in front of his truck," Angie pointed out. "There is a difference." Bubba had always called Erin Cupcake because he said she was so sweet.

"I don't care. I'm still gonna hurt him." Bubba made a move toward Hardy and Angie tried to hold him back.

"I'll give you the first one, Bubba, but that's it." Hardy rubbed his jaw with murder in his eye.

The door opened again, and Wyatt and Peyton came in. Wyatt took the situation in at a glance. "What's going on?"

Bubba looked at Wyatt. "Hardy hurt Cupcake."

"It was an accident. A terrible accident, and Angie doesn't need to deal with this on top of everything else."

Her father got to his feet. "Son, the sheriff is right. This is not the time or the place for your anger. If you can't control yourself, then you need to go home."

Angie took a deep breath. "I would appreciate it if everyone went home. I need to focus on Erin, and I can't handle this bickering right now."

"We're not leaving you alone," Doris said. "This is a time when you need your family."

Angie remembered her mother saying the same words when Angie had been pregnant and Dennis had left her.

But Angie had refused to be browbeaten and treated like a child. She wouldn't allow it today, either.

Before she could say a word, Wyatt spoke up, "Maybe it's best if we let Angie have some quiet time. She'll call if she needs us." Wyatt knew the Wiznowski family and their constant squabbling.

Doris glared at Wyatt. "You may be the sheriff of Horseshoe and have control there, but you can't tell me what to do concerning my daughter. I am her mother."

"He might not be able to," her father spoke up, to everyone's surprise, "but I can. Let's go. Angie will call if she needs us."

"Willard—"

"You heard me, Doris."

Angie had had enough. She was worried out of her mind about what her daughter was going through at that precise moment and she couldn't take anymore. She bolted for the door and ran down the hall away from everybody.

She reached a nurse's station and stopped. "Do you know if Erin Wiznowski is still in surgery? I'm her mother."

The nurse looked at the computer screen and tapped a few keys. "Yes, she's still in surgery. Dr. Robbins will be out to speak to you when it's over."

"Can I wait somewhere closer?"

"Sure. There are a couple of chairs around the corner, not far from the operating room. I'll let Dr. Robbins know you're there."

"Thank you." She went around the corner and sank into a chair. Taking several deep breaths, she tried to calm herself. So much had happened she didn't even know if that was possible.

"Angie."

She looked up to see Peyton standing there, a little unsure, which was out of character for her confident friend. "I brought this from your house." She handed Angie her purse.

"Thank you. I'd forgotten about it."

"Your phone's in there, and so is your charger."

Angie slipped the strap over her shoulder. "Is my family still here?"

"They were standing around the waiting room grumbling when I left." Peyton cocked her head. "Which is typical of the Wiznowskis."

"Yeah. That's a nice way to say it."

Peyton hugged her. "I'm a phone call away if you need anything."

"I know, and I'll call as soon as Erin is out of surgery."

"I can stay if—"

Angie shook her head. "No. Go home to your babies. I know no one understands how I'm feeling, but I really need to be alone."

"You got it. Talk to you tomorrow." Peyton walked down the hall. Angie wished her family was as easy to deal with.

She glanced at her watch and saw it was almost eight o'clock. Why wasn't the surgery over? She just couldn't stand the thought of Erin's perfect little body being operated on. Tears trickled from her eyes, and she brushed them away. More followed. *Oh, what the hell.* She needed to cry. That was the only way she was going to get this nightmare out of her system. The nervousness, the tension and the worry would still be there, but maybe she could cope better; at the moment she was losing a grip on everything she held dear.

"Angie."

She looked up, brushing tears away as quickly as she

could, and stared into those dark blue eyes that did a number on her self-control. Why couldn't he follow everyone's lead and leave?

He held a cup of coffee in each hand. "Thought you might need this."

She accepted the drink gratefully. "Thank you."

"Are you okay?"

"No. Erin's never been away from me except to spend a night at my mom's or Jody's, but I'm never far away. I need to hold my baby to know she's going to be fine. That's when I'll be okay." Her hands gripped the warm cup. "And I'll be much better once you get off the guilt trip, too. Please leave me in peace."

"Sorry—I can't do that until I know your daughter's okay."

"Her name is Erin," she said, sharper than she'd intended. Maybe because a father should know his child's name. And the father had a right to know he had a child.

How did she tell him that? How did she make up for ten years of keeping a secret without tearing Erin's world apart? And without shattering Hardy's?

She took a sip of the coffee and stared into the depths of the liquid, which was as dark as her soul. How had a good Catholic girl gone so wrong?

She cleared her throat. "Hardy…"

Chapter Three

Dr. Robbins came around the corner, stopping Angie. She ran to him. "How's my daughter?"

The doctor pulled off his surgical cap. "She's fine. Everything went smoothly. They're taking her to a room. You can get the number from the nurse."

"Oh, thanks."

"We'll go over her care first thing in the morning. She'll probably sleep most of the night. If she complains about pain, I've left something on order for her."

"Thank you." Angie hurried down the hall to the nurse's station. Hardy stared after her.

"She's really going to be fine," the doctor said to him.

"Yeah." He sighed, wondering if she would recover completely. "She has a lot of weeks of healing ahead, though."

"Kids are tough, and she'll bounce back quickly." The doctor nodded and followed Angie.

Hardy stood there feeling something he couldn't explain. The little girl was going to be okay, so he should go home. His father and Olivia were waiting to hear from him. But for some reason, he couldn't make himself leave the hospital. Maybe it was the worry on Angie's face and the fact that he'd caused it.

He saw Wyatt walking toward him, and he went to meet him.

"What are you still doing here?" he asked his friend.

Wyatt handed him his truck keys. "Peyton and I brought your truck so you'll have a way to get home."

"Ah, man, thanks. It hasn't crossed my mind yet that I don't have a ride."

"How's Erin?"

"She's out of surgery, and Angie has gone to be with her."

Wyatt removed his hat and scratched his head. "I wish she'd let someone stay with her, but she's one stubborn woman."

"Her family is supervocal, and I can see how they'd suck the energy right out of her."

Wyatt smiled. "They're a lively bunch, for sure." His friend looked at him. "Bubba didn't mean anything. He just loves his niece."

"I know that." Hardy rubbed his sore jaw. The punch was nothing compared to what Angie's daughter had suffered. He'd injured a child. He was still grappling with that.

"If you're leaving, I'll walk you out."

"Um…I'm going to stick around for a bit. I want to make sure everything's okay with the little girl."

"It was an accident, Hardy. I was there, so stop blaming yourself."

Hardy swiped a hand through his hair. "Tell that to my stomach."

"It'll get better." Wyatt patted him on the shoulder. "I'll catch you tomorrow."

Hardy tossed his coffee cup in a trash can and went to the nurse's desk to ask for the little girl's room number. She was in the pediatric ward, and it didn't take him long to find it. But he hesitated outside the door. Angie wasn't going to like him being there.

The hall was quiet and the lights had been dimmed for the night. Parents were with their children. He should leave and come back tomorrow. But he couldn't do that. He pushed the door open slightly.

Angie had a chair pulled close to the bed, and she was sitting in it, stroking her daughter's hair back from her forehead. The light was low, but he could see her clearly. She looked so different from that young, innocent girl she'd been a long time ago.

There was nothing remarkable about Angie's looks— she had golden-brown eyes, sandy-brown hair and a smooth complexion. Back then she'd been slim. Now her figure was more mature, and her hair was different, too. Evidently, her beautician sisters had highlighted it or something because it was more blond than brown now. She wore it in a ponytail with several strands curling around her face.

Yet Angie had a special quality that endeared her to everyone. When she talked, she spoke with a smile in her voice. She was open, honest and sweet. Everybody liked her. He was no exception.

The little girl stirred, and Angie was on her feet. An IV was still in the child's arm. Angie leaned down and whispered, "Erin, baby, Mama's here."

"Mama?"

"Yes. I'm right here."

"I...I feel funny." The tiny voice was soft and weak, and Hardy's stomach tightened like a balled fist.

"You've been in an accident, baby."

"What...happened?"

"You were running after your beach ball and—"

"Yeah. I didn't want it to go into Mrs. Wimby's yard... 'cause...she keeps things."

Angie kissed the girl's forehead. "I know, baby. Go back to sleep and we'll talk about it tomorrow."

"Have to get my ball, Mama, to go on our trip."

"Shh. Go back to sleep. Mama's here."

"My head hurts."

"I'll get the nurse."

Erin's eyes opened wide. "Where...where are we?"

"In the hospital."

"Why?" The little girl began to cry, and Hardy's stomach clamped that much tighter.

"Shh, baby. You're okay. Please don't cry."

The girl closed her eyes and drifted into a drug-induced sleep. Hardy stepped away from the door and sank into a chair in the hall. The girl wasn't okay. She was in pain. He took a couple of deep breaths, knowing the knot in his gut wasn't going to go away for a while. He was so angry with himself. It was a neighborhood with children. He should've been more careful. He should have—

He heard them before he saw them. Loud voices. Angry voices. Could only belong to Wiznowskis. It was the twins. There was no mistaking them. Colorful and flashy were their trademarks. He never could tell them apart, so he'd stopped trying.

One had on at least three-inch red clogs with a short skirt and a tank top. The other had on orange high heels, shorts and a gypsy-type blouse. Both wore necklaces, bracelets and earrings that jangled when they walked. Their hair color seemed to change weekly. Today one was a blonde with a bluish tint. The one in shorts had black hair with orangey highlights.

"She's going to be pissed," the one in the shorts said.

"So? I can be pissed, too," the other replied.

"AnaMarie said we should respect her wishes."

The blond-haired one laughed. "Since when do we listen to AnaMarie? She's an old fart."

"She's two years older than us."

"Do you have to argue about everything?"

"It's not me. It's you."

"Yeah, right."

They both stopped when they saw him. The one with the black hair stepped closer. "What are you still doing here? Haven't you done enough?"

He got to his feet, really not in the mood for another round with the Wiznowskis. "Making sure everyone is okay."

The blonde's eyes narrowed. "Does Angie know you're out here?"

"No."

"Then you'd better leave."

He glanced from one to the other. "You know, I can never tell you two apart, so you'll have to introduce yourselves. I'd really like to know who I'm talking to."

"I'm Mary Patricia—Patsy," the black-haired one said.

"And I'm Mary Margaret, but everyone calls me Peggy."

"Well, Peggy, I'm not going anywhere until that little girl is better."

Peggy jammed a finger into her chest. "We'll take care of Erin. We've always helped Angie with our little angel. Your presence here only complicates things. Get my drift?"

"Not really. Your sister asked for some time alone with her daughter."

"Ah." Patsy waved a hand at him. "She was just upset. She needs us like she did when that bastard left her."

"Don't you think someone should call the little girl's father?" Angie had been very evasive when he'd asked about him, but if it were his kid, he'd want to know. He was sure the man felt the same way.

Patsy got into his face. "I think you're sticking your nose in where it doesn't belong."

"We can discuss this all day and all night, but my position is not changing."

Angie stepped into the hall, interrupting the heated conversation. "What are y'all doing here? I could hear you in the room."

Patsy approached her sister. "Don't go all mama bear on us. You didn't really think we'd leave, did you?" She held up a bag. "We went to get you something to eat."

"Thanks, but I'm not hungry."

Peggy hugged Angie. "How's Erin?"

"She woke up for a second and said her head hurt. I called a nurse, and they're bringing her something. She's really confused right now, I think—the fewer people she sees, the better it is for her."

"Come on, Angie. We're her aunties," Patsy said. "Let us just see her for a second so we can sleep tonight."

Angie held up one finger. "One minute. Visiting hours are over. You have to make it quick, and please do not wake her."

Patsy and Peggy hurried inside the room. That left him and Angie staring at each other. The same old message flashed in her eyes, and it didn't take her long to say it. "Why are you still here?"

Her voice was tired and a little sad. He felt guilty for upsetting her more than he already had.

Patsy and Peggy came out, wiping tears from their eyes.

"She's so pale." Peggy grabbed a tissue out of her huge purse.

Angie visibly swallowed. "Yes. She's had a horrific afternoon and…"

Angie stopped speaking as AnaMarie came toward them with a small suitcase in her hand.

"Well, if it isn't Ms. Old Fart," Patsy quipped. "I thought we were supposed to respect Angie's wishes."

"I should have known you two wouldn't listen."

AnaMarie and Hardy were the same age and in the same class in school. He liked her. She always had a lot of common sense, but she was very quiet and shy. Angie was like that, too.

AnaMarie and her mother, along with the grandmother, ran a bakery. Hardy used to go in there a lot, as did everyone in Horseshoe. When Angie had come back from Temple, he'd heard, she'd taken over the business end. She had an office inside the shop, so he didn't go in as much to avoid seeing her. Their encounters were stilted and awkward, and he never knew what to say to her. He just had an enormous guilt that he couldn't shake.

The bakery was the busiest place in town, and people came from all over to sample the kolaches, pies, cakes, cookies and every other imaginable sweet. The shop had been in the same family for as long as Hardy could remember. The Wiznowskis were well-known in Horseshoe. Bubba owed a gas station and wrecker service. Willard had a blacksmith shop and the twins operated a beauty shop that was called Talk of the Town. It was aptly named, as most rumors were started there. Angie also took care of their books and did taxes for just about everyone in Horseshoe.

"I brought you a change of clothes, toiletries and something to sleep in," AnaMarie said. "I'm prepared to stay, too. You need someone here."

"Thanks." Angie took the suitcase from her. "But no.

You have to open the bakery in the morning and I'm fine because Erin's going to be okay."

"Tomorrow is Sunday, and we're not open on Sunday," AnaMarie reminded her.

"I'm sorry." Angie touched her forehead. "I'm a little rattled."

"That's understandable. How's Erin?"

"She's a little restless, but the surgery went well."

Footfalls sounded again on the tiled floor, and they looked up to see Willard and Doris walking toward them.

"I had to come back," Doris said as she reached Angie. She gave Hardy a sharp glance but didn't say anything. "I can't rest until I know my granddaughter's okay."

"I tried, Angie," her father said. "But I was worried, too."

Angie hugged her parents. "Erin's going to be fine. You can see her for a minute."

No one said a word until they came out of the room. Doris dabbed at her eyes with a tissue. "My poor baby. Angie, I'll stay the night so someone is here with you."

"No, Mama. Everyone needs to go home. I can take care of Erin."

"I called Dale and Dorothy and told them what happened, and they send their love and prayers."

"Thank you, Mama."

A nurse came down the hall with a syringe in her hand. She glared at everyone. "Visiting hours are over. Y'all will have to leave."

"They're going," Angie replied. She followed the nurse into the room.

The family walked off without a backward glance, and Hardy thought that was just as well. Enough had been said today. He stretched his tired shoulders and moved down the hall so the nurse wouldn't see him. When the nurse came out of Erin's room, Hardy slipped in.

"Hardy." Angie sighed. "You have to leave."

He stared at the girl in the bed. Her skin was as white as the sheet. He wondered if she was really okay. Maybe that was why he couldn't leave. His shoulders drooped with fatigue.

He glanced at Angie's worried face. "You have to call her father. He needs to know his child is hurt, no matter what your relationship is with him."

"I told you, it's none of your business." The smile in her voice was gone, replaced by the same fatigue he was feeling.

"Patsy said he left you, but…"

Angie leaned down and kissed her daughter, then walked into the hall, making sure the door was slightly opened. She sat in one of the chairs. "Okay. If you want to have this conversation now, let's have it."

He sat beside her, his elbows on his knees and his hands clasped together. "I'm not upsetting you on purpose."

"It feels like it."

The hall was dimly lit, and the only sounds were the beeps of a machine and murmurs coming from the nurse's station. He wished he could articulate what he was feeling, but he was having a hard time explaining it to himself.

"I'm really sorry about today, Angie. I'd give my life for it not to have happened. I should have been more careful. I should have—"

"Do you believe that things happen for a reason?"

He was taken aback for a moment. "I suppose. I've never really thought about it."

Angie wore shorts and she rubbed her hands down

her bare thighs. He couldn't tear his eyes away from the nervous action, trying not to remember the touch of her silky skin against his.

"What does this have to do with your ex-husband?"

"Nothing. It has everything to do with you."

"I get I'm being a little pushy, but I injured the man's child and I'd like to apologize. I'd like to do something."

"Dennis is not part of our lives and he wouldn't appreciate your apology or your gesture."

"I don't get that. He has a daughter."

She moved restlessly. "I could say again that it doesn't concern you, but I'm tired and weary of carrying a load so heavy it has finally brought me to my knees."

Hardy didn't know what to say. He'd spent many hours in a courtroom with the right response ready at every moment, but here in the hallway he didn't have a clue how to respond.

"When I was eighteen, I was very naive and believed in love." She took a deep breath. "I believed in love so strongly I knew the moment we made love you'd fall deeply in love with me. How stupid was that?"

"I'm sorry I hurt you." They were the only words he could push through his dry throat. She was sincere and honest, and he hated himself at that moment. Hated what had happened between them. Hated he'd destroyed her belief in love.

"And I'm sorry I believed in a love that didn't exist, but only in my dreams."

"Angie…"

She held up a hand. "No. Let me say what I have to say because I know you're not going to stop until you hear the whole story."

"What story?" He didn't understand what she was

talking about. "We made a bad decision, and we both realized that afterward."

"You did. I thought I loved you. Even though it was a teenage crush, my feelings were very real to me."

He clasped his hands until they were numb. The numbness spread to his wrist, his arms. "It's been so many years ago I don't understand why we're talking about it now."

"You said our night together was a mistake."

"You agreed."

She shook her head. "I didn't say much of anything. You did all the talking. It wasn't a mistake to me. It will never be."

He swallowed hard. "You were so young. You had your whole life ahead of you and—"

"You never asked how I felt. It was all about you and what you'd perceived you'd done."

He drew a long breath. "What does this have to do with your ex-husband not being here?"

"I made bad choices when I was eighteen, but I thought I had made the right choices at the time. Looking back, I can see I was desperately trying to save my pride because that was all I had left."

He didn't say anything because he was completely lost. He had no idea what she was talking about. Yet he could clearly hear in her voice that he'd hurt her. He didn't know how to make that right. They had both moved on to different lives. He saw no reason to dredge it all up again. He had to say something, though.

"You were very young, and I think your feelings for me were blown out of proportion."

"You could be right about that, because those feelings soon faded." She sat up straight and wrapped her arms around her waist. "I felt very foolish."

"Angie, what are you trying to tell me?"

"Like I said, I believe things happen for a reason. You came around that corner at that precise moment and literally crashed into everything I had been keeping a secret for ten years."

"What...what are you saying?"

She didn't answer for a moment, and he sensed she was gauging her next words. "I'm saying Erin's father doesn't need to be notified because he's already here."

"What?"

"You're Erin's father."

Chapter Four

The hallway went dark. Completely. Like a rabbit hole. And he was tumbling down, down, down. The only sound he heard was his heart slamming against his ribs in panic.

You're Erin's father.

He'd known.

Somewhere in his subconscious, he'd known. That was why he couldn't leave the hospital. Angie had desperately wanted to get rid of him, and that had triggered his lawyer's antenna. True, he'd just run into her child with his truck, but he'd sensed it was more than that. So he'd kept prodding. Kept insisting. Kept questioning.

Oh, my God! He'd hit his own child.

How could that be?

He rose to his feet like a drunk who'd spent too many hours in a bar. His head hurt. His nerves were shaky, and he couldn't focus beyond the now.

You're Erin's father.

"We used protection. How could she be mine?" He was still holding on to the belief that it wasn't possible he had a child and didn't know.

"Condoms are not one hundred percent foolproof. You should know that."

He shook his head. "No…no…" But from her steady

gaze, he knew she wasn't lying. "How could you do this to me?" burst from his throat.

Her head down, her hands clasped in her lap, she replied in a voice that seemed to echo through the hole in his heart. "How was I supposed to tell you when you weren't here?"

"My father knew how to get in touch with me. You could have asked him."

"I did. I made the trip twice, and both times he thought I wanted to speak to Rachel. He called her in Paris so we could talk. The second time Rachel didn't answer and I asked about you. He told me you were engaged and getting married around Christmas. He added that you'd found the perfect wife for your political career. I couldn't tell you after that. I could have ruined your life."

"That's supposed to make it okay?"

Angie kept her head down. "Of course not."

"Why? Why would you keep it from me all these years?" He tried to keep his voice calm but feared he'd failed. He sounded like a drill sergeant.

"If you remember, you were in Europe. When I realized you were back and living in Houston, I tried your cell number and it wasn't working anymore."

"It was stolen in Paris, and I got a new one."

"I was young and didn't know what to do. You didn't love me, and the fact that I was pregnant would only wreck your life, your career. That's the way I saw it then."

"So you thought it was better for your daughter and me to never know about each other. Wait. I've been back for over two years in Horseshoe and in that time you couldn't find a moment to tell me the truth?"

She heaved a sigh. "I tried. Three times, if you'll remember."

"When?"

"You were home for a while before I even knew you were back in Horseshoe, but when I saw you talking to Wyatt outside the courthouse, I left the bakery and walked over. I asked if you had a few minutes to talk, and you looked at your watch and said you had a meeting in fifteen minutes and that you would catch me later. I waited, but you never made any move to get in touch with me."

He remembered. "You didn't make it sound important. I guess I forgot."

"No, you didn't forget. You just didn't want to talk to me because there were two other times I tried to tell you and you brushed me off."

He frowned. "When?"

"You were busy campaigning for the D.A. job, but I hung in there, wanting you to know you had a child. You were getting in your truck at the courthouse, and I stopped you and asked if you had a few minutes. A blonde walked up. You know those blondes you're known for dating—a model type, perfect body. And once again you said you'd catch me later. Still, I didn't give up. At Wyatt and Peyton's at Christmas I asked again if we could talk. And you know what you did, Hardy?"

He clamped his jaw tight because he had no defense.

"You introduced me to your new girlfriend and you quickly forgot my request. I didn't know how else I was supposed to tell you when you clearly didn't want to talk to me. So don't stand there and point the finger unless you are completely blameless."

He wasn't. He knew that, and he was struggling with the consequences of his actions. He remembered all those times she'd approached him and, God help him, he'd thought she had wanted to start their relationship over again. How could he be so blind? So self-centered?

He took a moment to gather his thoughts and tried to find some normalcy in this awful day. Tried to find a reason why he'd shut her out.

He said the first thing that came into his mind. "Why did you marry someone else?"

"My friend Dennis found me crying one day after class. He wanted to know what was wrong, and I told him what I hadn't told anyone else. We studied together and went to the movies a couple of times. We were good friends, but Dennis wanted it to be more. His solution was we'd just get married and he'd raise the child as his. Out of fear of my mother's wrath, I agreed."

"What happened to the marriage?"

She twisted her fingers together. "When I was about seven months, Dennis asked if I loved him. I knew what he wanted to hear, but I couldn't say the words. He said he'd hoped that I would grow to love him and it was clear that was never going to happen. We ended the marriage amicably. I took back my maiden name. He later married someone else and now has two children."

"Your sister said he left you."

"He did. I just never told them the reason why because then I'd have to tell them the truth about Erin." She took a breath. "At the time I took full responsibility for what happened between us and planned to raise my child alone."

"She wasn't just yours."

Angie buried her face in her hands, and he stilled himself against the emotions churning in him. She raised her head. "How would you have felt if I'd told you back then?"

He swung away and jammed both hands through his hair, irritated he couldn't respond with an honest heart. His marriage hadn't lasted. It hadn't taken him long to figure out he wasn't in love with Lisa. But still, that didn't make what Angie had done right.

He swung around. "I would've taken care of my kid. She would have known that I was her father. Now I'm a stranger to her. And that's your fault, Angie."

"Yes. It's my fault," she said without offering one word in her defense. That irritated him even more.

His insides rumbled like thunder before a storm, and any minute Angie was going to feel the full impact of his wrath. To stop the rage building in him, he walked into his daughter's room and stared at the girl in the bed. Her head tilted to the left and her brown hair clumped around her face. One side of her face was blue, and the white sterile strips on her forehead stood out vividly. She wore a pediatric pink gown that made her skin look even paler. His throat closed up.

My daughter.

Was she okay?

He'd injured his child.

Thoughts pounded at him like hail from the storm brewing in him. He had to get away and make sense of everything. He turned, and Angie stood there, watching him.

"We need to talk," she said in a low voice.

"I don't want to hear anything else," he told her. "Nothing you can say is going to make this better. I have to get away from you. From myself."

"Hardy, please. I need to know—"

He walked out the door and down the hall. He had no idea where he was going until he reached the entrance. The parking lot loomed in front of him, and he did a quick scan to locate his truck. After climbing inside, he started the engine and headed for somewhere. Or nowhere. He wasn't quite sure, but any place was better than dealing with a woman who had deceived him.

Angie. Sweet, irresistible Angie had just shattered his heart. And there was no way to forgive that.

Ever.

ANGIE STARED OUT the window toward Horseshoe. It was dark, but she knew the direction.

She touched the windowpane and the coolness of the glass shot all the way to her heart. She was cold and empty. Somewhere deep inside she found the courage she'd been running on for years. It was like high octane keeping her going. But being strong had cost her more than she'd ever imagined.

She exhaled deeply, turned back to Erin and sat in the chair by the bed, her hand stroking Erin's face.

After Dennis had left, she hadn't known how to tell her mother that the marriage was over. Being a strong Catholic, her mother didn't believe in divorce. So, with her stubborn pride intact, she'd had Erin alone, but after the birth she'd called Patsy and Peggy. She'd needed someone. They got her through it, and then she'd gone home to her parents.

There had been tons of questions from her mother, but her pit-bull sisters had fielded every one of them. And she'd let them protect her until she found the courage once again to stand on her own. It hadn't been easy, and now she was about to lose it all.

She laid her head on the bed, tears rolling from her eyes. Everyone thought Dennis was Erin's father, even her family. She'd told no one, not even Dennis, that Hardison Hollister was the father of her baby. That had been her secret.

Looking at her precious daughter, she had one thought.

It was over. Her secret wasn't a secret anymore. Hardy knew he was Erin's father. She should feel some sort of relief, but the boulder on her chest felt that much heavier. Because it really wasn't over. The worst was yet to come.

HARDY'S HEAD POUNDED, and he cursed under his breath. Where was he? It was dark, and he was sitting outside on a bench. A warm breeze touched his face and ruffled his hair. Reaching up to brush it out of his eyes, he realized he had a bottle in his hand. A whiskey bottle.

Just what he needed. He took a swig. Oh, yeah, Tennessee whiskey. It should solve all his problems, or maybe just drown them.

Through the pounding he kept hearing *You're Erin's father*.

He took another swallow, but the sound wouldn't go away. *Damn!* He needed more booze.

"Hardy, is that you?"

Hardy blinked and saw at least two Wyatt Carsons standing there. He knew it was him because the moonlight reflected off the badge on his shirt.

"Yeah."

"What are you doing sitting on the bench in front of the courthouse?"

"Hell, I don't know." He turned the bottle up again.

"Are you drunk?"

"Good guess. You're not the sheriff for nothing."

Wyatt sat beside him. "Are you drinking that straight?"

"Straight as an arrow to my gut, and I'm waiting for the numbness to knock me on my ass."

"What's wrong with you? I know it's been a rough day, but I've never seen you drink like this and I've known you all of my life."

"You know me pretty well, huh?"

"Pretty good." Wyatt nodded.

"Do you know I have a kid?"

"What?"

"I have a kid, and I found out tonight."

"You're talking out of your head." Wyatt stood. "Let's go over to the jail and I'll make some coffee and you can sober up. Then you can tell me what's going on."

"I'm telling you now. Damn it! Can't you hear me?"

"The whole town can hear you, and I don't think you want them to see the D.A. drunk on his ass."

"Like I give a damn." He tipped up the bottle again.

Wyatt jerked it out of his hand. "You've had enough."

Hardy sat with his elbows on his knees, his face buried in his hands. "I have a kid, Wyatt. A kid I know nothing about."

Wyatt sat down again. "Are you serious?"

"As serious as I've ever been."

"How did you find this out?"

Hardy ran his hands up his face, trying to wipe away her voice. But it was right there, taunting him. He exhaled deeply. "She told me."

"Who told you?"

"You'd never guess in a million years."

Wyatt sighed. "Let's go get some coffee."

"Angie."

Complete silence followed the word, and he could see his friend was flabbergasted.

"Are you talking about Angie Wiznowski?"

"Is there another Angie you know?"

"You mean…?"

The storm that had been brewing in him suddenly hit. He jumped to his feet, which was a trick because the world suddenly tipped. His stomach roiled and didn't give him any time. He threw up everything he had in him, holding on to a tree. Sinking to his knees, he felt like the lowest scum who had ever walked on earth.

Wyatt put an arm around his waist and helped him to his feet. They made their way to the sheriff's office.

Stuart, a deputy, opened the door, and Hardy headed for the bathroom. After rinsing out his mouth and washing his face, he took a moment to gather his composure. He walked into Wyatt's office and sank into a chair. A cup of coffee was pushed into his hand, and he held it as if to steady the world around him. After downing two cups, his mind began to clear, but his head felt as big as the Alamo.

Wyatt sat in his leather chair across from him. "Stuart, you can go home. I got it."

Stuart was thin and wiry and known to have the curiosity of a gossip columnist. "I can stay, Sheriff."

"Thanks, Stu, but Lamar will be in soon, so go home early."

"Okay." Stu ambled slowly to the door, obviously hoping to hear a tidbit of gossip that would be all over Horseshoe in minutes.

"How did you know I was at the courthouse?" Hardy asked. "It's still dark."

"Stuart saw you drive up on the curb and watched you for a little bit, and then he called me. He was afraid to approach you. You know, being the D.A. and all, who is known as a respectable man around town."

Hardy winced. "Okay. Drive it in with a sledgehammer."

Wyatt got up and brought him another cup of coffee. "Talk, because you weren't making much sense earlier."

He sipped the dark brew. "I'm Erin's father. I wonder how long I'll have to say that before I'll really believe it."

Wyatt tapped a pencil on the desk. "You'll have to tell

me how that's possible. Angie married some guy she met in Temple. He left her, and she brought the baby home to Horseshoe. How do you fit into this picture? You were in Houston, I believe."

"It happened before I went to Houston and before Dad and I took Rachel to Paris."

"And…" Wyatt prompted.

"After our mother was killed, Rachel had a hard time. She was restless and very unhappy. Then she made friends with Angie, who was as calm as a summer's day. She was a good influence for my sister. Dad threw Rachel a big going-away party and had all her friends over. Angie was there." He stared down into the coffee cup, not really wanting to share this with his friend. But he had to tell someone. It didn't take him long to tell about the summer with Angie and what he'd found at the party when he'd gotten home. He took a swallow of coffee to bolster his courage. "I let Angie sleep it off because I knew how her mother was. The next morning things happened that I wish had never happened. She was too young, and I should've known better, but I can't go back and change it."

"You didn't see her after that?"

"I saw her in town a few days before we left for Europe. I told her how sorry I was and wished her all the best for the future."

"It never crossed your mind she could be pregnant?"

"We used protection."

"Come on, Hardy."

He ran his hands up his face. "I'm so angry and I want to blame her, but—"

"Did she give a reason for not telling you?"

He set his cup on the desk. "Yeah. I was in Europe at first, but when she heard I was back, she approached my dad and he told her I was engaged. She didn't want to ruin my life. That's rich, huh?"

"Sounds like Angie to me. She doesn't like to hurt people."

Hardy stood and swiped a hand through his disheveled hair. "Well, she hurt me."

Wyatt leaned back in his chair. "Did she give a reason for not telling you once you returned to Horseshoe?"

Guilt pounded at him with the force of a baseball bat. "She tried, but I brushed her off every time."

"Why would you do that?"

He took a ragged breath. "That's hard to explain, but I didn't want to get involved with Angie again."

"Why?"

"I'd rather not talk about it. First, I have to figure out a way to deal with all this anger inside me. And, yeah, a lot of it is at myself."

"My advice to you is to get over to the hospital and talk to Angie and be there for her and Erin. Put your hurt feelings aside and think about what Angie's going through now. Do you think you can do that?"

He looked at his friend through narrowed eyes. "You're taking her side."

"There are no sides here. You and Angie have to find a balance for Erin."

"I know that. But what do I do with all this anger?"

"Lay off the booze, for one thing. And take it one day at a time. Once you get to know Erin, she'll replace all that anger with love."

"How many times have I seen her at your house playing with Jody?"

"A lot."

"And I never suspected a thing. Remember that day she and Jody were playing hopscotch on the sidewalk and she fell and skinned her knee? I had just driven up. I picked her up and carried her into the house. She felt like a feather in my arms, a beautiful feather. I picked up my daughter, and I didn't even know she was mine. That's what makes me so angry. All the years I've missed and she was right under my nose. My child was there, and I never saw her."

Wyatt came around the desk and patted him on the shoulder. "Sorry, man. That's rough."

Hardy drew a deep breath. "I'd better go home, get cleaned up and see how my kid is doing. And I have Dad and Olivia to deal with. I bailed on them last night."

"Are you going to tell the judge?"

"I might wait before telling him. He'll want to rush in and cause all kinds of problems. Right now I'm just feeling my way and hoping to see and spend some time with my child."

"What about Olivia?"

"I don't know, Wyatt. She's not going to be happy, but I have a kid and I'm not walking away from her." He frowned. "Do you have any idea where my truck is?"

"You jumped the curb at the courthouse and it's parked half on, half off the lawn. The quicker you get it off, the better it will be for the gossip, because come daylight, your story is going to be all over town."

Hardy headed for the door. "Thanks, Wyatt."

"I take it the Wiznowskis don't know you're Erin's biological father."

He turned back. "I assume they think the ex is the father."

"If you think Bubba is hard to deal with, wait until the news spreads through the rest of the family. You'll have your hands full defending yourself."

"I hadn't thought of that, and I really don't care about

their reaction. I only care about getting to know my daughter."

"What made Angie tell you now?"

Hardy shrugged. "I kept pressing her about Erin's father. He needed to be there, and she was very evasive about him. Maybe she got tired of me pressuring her or maybe she just got tired of keeping her secret. I don't know. She just blurted it out."

"Good luck, man. I'm here if you need me."

"Thanks."

As he backed his truck off the lawn, he knew Wyatt was right. His name would be mud all over town. But he wasn't worried about that. The only worry he had was how to make a connection to a little girl he didn't even know.

Because he was her father.

Chapter Five

Hardy sped down the county blacktop to the Circle H Ranch. He drove under the wrought iron arch entrance and onto the graveled road that led to the colonial-style two-story house. Brown board fences bordered him on both sides. Live oaks graced the fence all the way to the house. In places their branches intertwined, giving a shady umbrella effect.

He swung into his parking spot in the detached garage. After walking through a breezeway into the kitchen, he found his dad, Mavis and Harvey Weltzen eating breakfast. Mavis had been the housekeeper for years and Harvey was the foreman of the ranch.

His dad looked up from his plate. "Where in the hell have you been?"

Judge Hardison Sr. was a barrel-chested man who exuded confidence and attitude. His booming voice was known to stop criminals in their tracks. Most people feared him because of his strong stance on crime and morality. There was no leeway, according to him.

"I told you, I was involved in an accident and I had to handle things."

"You should've been man enough to phone and let us know what was going on. We worried all night. Olivia's been calling and calling." His dad looked him up and down. "You look fine. What kind of accident?"

The criticism stung, and Hardy bit his tongue. "A little girl ran out in front of my truck and I hit her."

"Oh, my God!" Mavis covered her mouth with her hand in shock. "Is she okay?"

"She's in the hospital in Temple with a broken leg, some cracked ribs and a bruise on her head, but the doctor said she's going to be fine."

"Where did you hit this girl?" his dad asked in his most authoritative voice.

"On Magnolia Street. I was on my way home."

"Who is she?"

"Angie Wiznowski's daughter."

"Did Wyatt take a report?"

"Not yet, but I'm sure he will."

His dad pointed a finger at him. "Get this swept under the rug as fast as you can."

Hardy clenched his jaw. "I'm not sweeping anything under the rug. It was an accident. If people can't understand that, then they have a problem."

"Boy, you've got a lot to learn."

"I'm the D.A. of this county, and I will make sure that the legal procedure is followed, even when it includes me."

"If charges are filed, you can kiss that D.A. job goodbye and any chance of running for district judge will be gone. Talk to Angie. She's a sweet girl. She'll understand."

He turned toward the hallway. "I've got to go."

Hardy had spent years trying to live up to everything his father expected of him. But sometimes the pressure got to him.

"Your sister called last night."

He looked back. "How is she?" Rachel rarely phoned.

"Still trying to find the real Rachel teaching art in New York. I told her if she doesn't know who she is by now, she needs to stop looking and come home. Eleven years is long enough."

There were times when Hardy questioned his reasons for returning to Horseshoe. He'd had a good job in Houston at a top-notch law firm, and he should've stayed there. Because of his father's health, Hardy had come home to be there for him. Under doctor's orders, the judge had retired; his high blood pressure was out of control. The doctor had warned of a heart attack or a stroke. But if Hardy'd learned anything, he'd learned that Hardison Hollister Sr. never needed anyone.

"We're vaccinating calves today. You have time to help?"

"No, Dad. I told you. I'll be busy handling the accident and making sure the little girl's medical bills are paid."

His dad bobbed his head. "Yeah. Yeah. That's what you need to do. Put on a good front. Show everyone you're sorry. Just don't let this get out of control."

Hardy sighed. The situation was so far out of control he didn't know if he could ever gain any ground with Angie or his daughter. The thought of telling his dad the truth briefly floated to his mind. But he quickly regained his senses. His father would storm in like the National Guard, taking over Angie and the child and making sure she knew she was a Hollister. Hardy wasn't ready for that. Angie wasn't, either.

"I'll catch you later."

On his way to the stairs, the doorbell rang. "I'll get it," he shouted to Mavis. Olivia stood on the doorstep. She ran into his arms. Seeing her, Angie's words came back to him. Blonde. Model type. Perfect body. That explained Olivia to a T. Was she right? Did he only date one type of woman?

But there was more to Olivia than good looks. She was a trial lawyer and worked for a big firm in Austin.

"Are you okay?" She stroked his face. "You said you were in some kind of accident. Your text was really short, and I was worried."

"I'm fine." He kissed her hand and told her what had happened.

Her blue eyes widened. "Does your father know?" Her response threw him for a moment, but then Olivia and his father were on the same wavelength—motivated by Hardy's political career.

"Yes. Uh…we need to talk, but I don't have time right now. I have to get back to the hospital to make sure the girl is okay."

She reached up and kissed him. "That would be best. You don't want this to get out of hand."

He didn't respond. At the moment he was feeling a little empty and conflicted. He'd tell Olivia about Erin later. "I'll call you tonight."

Without another word he hurried to his room, showered and changed clothes and made his way back to the hospital. He had to know how his daughter was doing.

As he drove toward Temple, it hit him that he hadn't had any sleep. He had sobered up from a pretty bad drunken stupor. He wasn't in his twenties anymore, and the all-nighter would catch up with him sooner rather than later. But nothing was keeping him away from the hospital. This morning his daughter would be awake, and he had this urgency just to see her face—her animated face—so he could get a feel of who she really was.

He didn't allow himself to think of Angie. His anger toward her was still raw, but he had to be honest. She wasn't the only one to blame. He should've checked back with her. He knew that would weigh heavily on him in the days ahead, as would her earlier attempts to talk to him about the pregnancy.

His dad thought he should save his reputation, but Hardy was more concerned about trying to save his self-respect. He'd let Angie down, and he would think about that when his anger got the best of him.

As he neared Temple, his heart beat faster. In a few minutes, he would see his daughter.

And Angie.

What was he supposed to say to her now?

ANGIE WOKE UP with a start. She was still in the chair with her head resting on Erin's bed, one hand on Erin's stomach. The doctor said Erin would be fine, but she still had to feel her daughter's heartbeat just to make sure.

Around midnight, Erin had woken up crying and the nurse had injected something into the IV so she could rest. Angie brushed soft brown hair from Erin's warm forehead; some of it was caked with blood. The bruise was now almost black. That was going to take a while to heal. Her baby would be in some pain for several days, and Angie would do everything she could to ease the trauma Erin was going through.

Angie stood, stretched her aching shoulders and walked around to exercise her stiff legs. Light seeped in through the window. It was a new day, and Angie felt it was also a new beginning. She had no idea what Hardy was going to do now, but she had to be prepared. For herself. And Erin.

She took a shower and changed into capris and a sleeveless top, grateful AnaMarie had thought to bring them. After brushing her hair, she whipped it into a ponytail and went back to her daughter. Erin was still out. Angie paced around the room to keep from sitting and worrying. She dared not leave to go for coffee, but, oh, she needed some.

The door opened, and Hardy stood there with two cups in his hands, the same as last night. Her heart hammered loudly in her ears. They stared at each other for a long moment, neither knowing what to say.

His dark hair was slicked back, and worry mixed with anger slashed across the strong lines of his handsome face.

Finally, he held out one of the cups. "Thought you might need this."

Her hands closed around the offering without a second thought. "Thank you."

Hardy looked toward the bed. "Has she been awake?"

"Once, and they gave her something for pain. She should wake up anytime now."

He walked to the bed and stared at Erin. His sun-browned skin paled. "What day was she born? And where? There's so many things I don't know about her. All I know is she's Jody's best friend."

"Could we not get into this now, please?"

His eyes caught hers. "When, then? Another eleven years or so?"

The hurt in his eyes jolted her and a hollow feeling settled in her stomach.

"I'd rather not talk about this in front of her, even though she's asleep."

"I want her to know I'm her father."

Angie swallowed hard. "I'll tell her, but not until I know she can handle it. She's only ten years old. Her birthday was yesterday."

His eyes darkened. "Yesterday? I hit her on her birthday?"

"That's why all the cars were there. I gave her a big party."

"Oh, God." He looked at Erin again. "I've run out of ways to say I'm sorry. I've run out of ways to be angry and to justify all this. She's my kid, and you never told me. I'm struggling with that."

Her heart broke for what he was going through. For what she had caused him. And he was right. There was no other way to say *I'm sorry*. It had all been said. They had to go forward.

"Let's concentrate on Erin and her well-being. You're welcome to stay. I'll have to explain why you're here. She'll be surprised, but, please, let's take it slow. For Erin."

He kept staring at his child. "She looks nothing like me."

"Wait till she opens her eyes. They're dark blue like yours. I've worried for two years that you would notice that, but I don't think you ever saw her. I mean, really saw her. She was Jody's friend. That was it."

He glared at her. "And it made you happy that I never recognized my daughter?"

She bit her lip. "Honestly, no. It just made me very aware of the enormous secret I lived with, and I knew one day it would have to be told. For Erin's sake and yours."

"It didn't have to be a secret, Angie. That was your decision alone."

"Could we not do this now?" she asked again.

Erin stirred. "Mama," she whimpered.

Angie immediately went to her. "I'm here, baby."

"My head…hurts."

Angie stroked back Erin's hair with one hand and

pushed the nurse's button with the other. "You bumped your head. Remember?"

"No," Erin replied, and tears rolled from her eyes.

"Shh. It's okay. The nurse will be here in a minute."

"A nurse? Where are we?"

"We're in the hospital. Remember? You were in an accident."

"I want to go home," Erin cried.

A nurse came in. "Hi, Erin. You're awake. Are you in pain?"

Erin looked at Angie.

"Tell her how you feel, baby," Angie urged.

But Erin closed her eyes and turned her head.

Angie gently caressed her cheek. "Tell the nurse how you feel."

Erin opened her eyes. "My…my head hurts."

"How does your leg feel?" the nurse asked.

"I don't know," Erin murmured.

The nurse checked the IV and Erin's pulse, then took her blood pressure and temperature. She turned to Angie. "She's running a low-grade fever, but nothing to be alarmed about. I'll put something in the IV to relax her, but I'd like for her to stay awake for a little bit."

"Okay," Angie said. "But I don't want her to be in pain."

"Don't worry. We'll take care of that." The nurse disappeared out the door.

"What happened, Mama?" Erin asked, her voice shaky.

"You were in an accident. You were running after your beach ball and—"

"Yeah. I had to get it before it went into Mrs. Wimby's yard because she keeps whatever she finds in her yard."

Erin moved her head and winced. "I don't remember any more."

"It's okay, baby. We'll talk about it later," Angie told her. "Try to relax."

"Why does my head hurt?"

Angie swallowed again, trying to explain without upsetting her daughter. "You banged your head in the accident."

"Oh." Erin looked past Angie to Hardy. "What are you doing here, Mr. Hardy? Did I do something wrong?"

To Erin, Hardy represented the law.

Hardy stepped closer to the bed, his skin now a pasty white. "I'm sorry...Erin. I didn't see you. All of a sudden you were in front of my truck, and I slammed on the brakes. You didn't do anything wrong. I should have been more alert."

Erin glanced at Angie, not understanding what Hardy was talking about. "You ran out in front of Mr. Hardy's truck, and he hit you. That's why you're in the hospital. You hurt your head on the pavement and fractured your leg."

Erin's expression didn't change, and Angie wondered if she understood what she was trying to tell her. "Is it Monday?" Erin finally asked.

"No, baby. It's Sunday."

"Then tomorrow we're leaving on our trip?"

Angie chewed on her lip, knowing Erin wasn't going to take this well. They'd planned for two years to go to Disney World. How did she break her heart, especially when she was in pain? But she had to tell her the truth, which seemed hypocritical since she was keeping the biggest secret of all from her.

Angie stroked her daughter's hair once more. "No, baby, we won't be going to Disney World this summer.

We have to stay home so you can heal and learn to walk on your leg again."

"No! I can walk. I can walk. We can go."

Angie kissed Erin's cheek. "We'll go when you're better, but not tomorrow."

"That's not fair. I saved my money and..." Big tears rolled from her eyes again, and she cried openly, much as she had when she was younger.

Angie just held her, not knowing what else to say.

The doctor walked in. "Good morning."

Erin burrowed against Angie.

"Not a good morning, huh?" The doctor walked to the bed to check Erin's leg. He pinched her toes to check for blood circulation, and then he checked the bandage on her hip. From there he looked at the bruise on her forehead.

"She's complaining about her head hurting," Angie told him.

"Is that what the tears are about?"

"No. We had a trip planned for Disney World and now we can't go."

"I'm sorry," he said, still looking at Erin.

"I want to go home," Erin said.

"Sorry, but I'd like to keep you for a few more days. You have to learn to walk on crutches, and we want to keep an eye on the bruise on your forehead."

"Crutches?" Erin wailed. "I don't need them. I can walk."

Dr. Robbins shook his head. "Not for about six weeks."

Erin looked at Angie. "We have to do what the doctor says so you can get better," she tried to reassure her daughter.

Erin didn't say anything. She just seemed to sink farther into the bed, and Angie's heart ached.

Angie followed the doctor to the door, then realized

Hardy was behind her. She'd almost forgotten he was in the room.

"I'm worried about her head," Angie said.

"It's a bad bruise, but we've run all the tests and everything is fine. She just needs time to heal."

"How long will she have to stay here?"

"Maybe a week. If she's feeling okay, the therapist will get her up on crutches this afternoon to teach her how to use them. But I don't want to push it if her head is still hurting. The nurse will remove the IV this morning. She'll bounce back quickly, Ms. Wiznowski. We've taped her fractured ribs. The nurse will show you how to remove the bandage to bathe her. They're tiny fractures. At her two-week checkup, we'll do more X-rays and I'll probably remove the tape. Try not to worry. I'm sorry about the trip, but there will be other ones. If anything changes, the nurse will call me." He looked over Angie's shoulder to Hardy. "Relax and she'll relax. Have a good day."

"Mama," Erin called.

Angie went to her daughter. "What?"

"Can I have something to drink?"

"What do you want?" Hardy asked. "You name it and I'll get it."

Erin giggled. That was a good sign. She was bouncing back.

"Some juice. And ice cream."

Angie shook her head. "Juice and breakfast."

"You want ice cream? You're getting ice cream," Hardy said, and walked out of the room.

Angie quickly followed him. "Hardy, you can't give her everything she wants."

"The first thing my child asks for is ice cream and

she's going to get it, breakfast or no breakfast. That's the way it is, Angie."

She threw up her hands. "Okay. But remember, it's only seven o'clock."

"Doesn't matter." He stepped closer to her, and a light, musky scent drifted to her. Almost eleven years, and that scent always reminded her of him, his touch, that night and everything that happened that had changed her life. "Before this week is over, she will know she's my daughter."

Holding on to her pride, she asked, "Are you prepared for her reaction?"

He lifted an eyebrow. "Are you?"

No, she wasn't, but she wouldn't admit that to Hardy. By the end of the week, her daughter could hate her and the walls of her life would come tumbling down.

Chapter Six

The next few days were a tug-of-war between Angie and Hardy. She didn't expect him to be at the hospital every day, and it was starting to get on her nerves. Erin recovered quickly, as the doctor had said she would, and she learned to use the crutches even quicker. The bruise on her head started to heal, and she didn't complain about headaches anymore. She was back to her cheery self, especially with all the attention she was getting from the family and her friends. And Hardy.

The room was full of stuffed animals, toys, balloons and flowers. Angie stopped telling him it was too much because he never listened. A showdown was coming soon.

Erin was going home tomorrow, and Angie was hoping for some sort of normalcy. That might be wishful thinking on her part because they were far, far away from normal.

Erin played on Hardy's phone, and he sat watching her, enthralled.

"I can't wait to get a phone," Erin said. "Jody and I are going to get one at the same time. I want a pink one. She wants a blue one. It'll be so cool."

"I'll buy you one," Hardy said without even looking at Angie, without even thinking she might disapprove.

Erin stopped poking the keypad. "You can't buy me a phone, Mr. Hardy." Erin looked at her mother. "Can he?"

"No, sweetie. Remember? When Jody turns eleven, you both get a phone. Since she's three months older, we agreed you could get one then. And we're not changing the plan now." She gave Hardy a sharp stare.

Erin raised a fist in the air. "Mama rules." She handed Hardy his phone. "Besides, you've given me all this stuff." She glanced around the roomful of goodies. "You didn't hit me on purpose or anything." Erin dropped her voice to sound like the sheriff. "You didn't do anything wrong, so you are now free to go." She ruined the seriousness of the declaration by giggling.

Hardy stared at her with the same enthralled expression. "So I'm forgiven?"

Erin nodded. "But you can always buy me ice cream."

"Deal, but I'd still like to come by and check on you."

"Sure." Erin bobbed her head. "I'll be home mending." She made a face.

Hardy kept staring at Erin, and Angie could see it was killing him that she didn't know she was his daughter. She felt a stab of regret like so many she'd had over the past ten years. Her heart should be a pincushion by now.

The move home went smoothly. Hardy was there to help her get Erin into the SUV, and then he carried Erin into the house and into her bedroom. The whole family was there, and it turned into a three-ring circus, a juggling angry-brother act, a fire-eating grandma and twin comedians determined to make Erin laugh. Hardy stayed through it all. Long after everyone had left, he was still there.

Angie sat in the kitchen, wondering how to tell Hardy it was time for him to go home. There didn't seem to be a proper way, so she played it by ear and prayed for strength to get through the next few hours.

HARDY FLIPPED THROUGH the channels, looking for something for Erin to watch. Erin lay on the sofa, propped up with pillows, and he was at her beck and call. He would do anything for her. It amazed him he had these fatherly instincts come out of nowhere.

"Tell me when you find something you like and I'll stop," he said, zooming through a ton of channels.

"Oh," she cried excitedly, pointing to the TV. "Let's watch *The Big Bang Theory*. It's funny."

"*The Big Bang* it is." He sat in a chair and listened to his daughter giggle, and it was the most beautiful sound. Every time she looked at him with those deep blue eyes, he was captivated.

Angie came in looking tired, and his heart twisted. She'd had a rough few days, and his presence made it worse. On one hand, he couldn't feel sorry for that because she'd caused it. But deep inside, he knew he did.

"Sweetie, it's time for bed," she told Erin. "You don't want to overdo it on your first day home."

Erin scrunched up her face. "But Mr. Hardy and I haven't had ice cream yet."

Hardy got up. "I put ice-cream bars in the freezer."

Erin raised her arms in the air. "Yay!"

Hardy offered Angie a bar, but she refused, a stubborn expression etched across her face.

After they finished their treat, he said, "Now, peanut, it's time for bed." He had started calling her that in the hospital because she'd looked so tiny in the hospital bed. She seemed to like it.

He handed Erin the crutches, and she stood up and wobbled a little. "I can carry you to the bed."

"No," Angie immediately protested. "Erin has to learn to use the crutches, and she knows how to use them."

"Mama's tough," Erin said, making her way into her pink-and-white bedroom.

Erin already had her gown on because Angie had helped her with her bath earlier. "Say good-night to Mr. Hardy," Angie instructed while getting Erin comfortable.

"Good night, Mr. Hardy, and thanks for the ice cream and for helping Mama get me into the house. You rock."

"Good night, peanut. I'll see you tomorrow." He wanted so badly to step over and kiss her good-night, and it took a lot of willpower not to do that.

Angie walked him to the door as if she couldn't get rid of him fast enough.

"It's time to tell her."

"I disagree. We need to talk first."

He sighed. "That's not a surprise."

"Give her time to heal before we throw this at her."

He stared into her eyes. "No, we're going to do this just as soon as possible."

"Are you even thinking about Erin? Or is it just about you and your pride?"

"Angie…"

"Have you told your father or Olivia about your daughter?"

"I haven't had time."

"Until you tell them, until you're prepared to welcome her into your life, you're not telling her. She's still healing. She needs time."

"Don't you mean you need time?"

There was a long pause. "You used to not be so pigheaded."

"And you were sweet and honest," he countered and watched the color flood her face. Back then it had been easy to make her blush. Maybe some things just never changed. "Angie, I want her to know I'm her father." His voice softened when he saw the look in her eyes.

"Okay, but we need to talk first."

"About what? Haven't we covered it all?"

"No. We haven't talked about anything but her well-being. We need to talk about what happens after we tell her."

"Okay. Let's talk."

"I'm too tired to get into it now." She tucked a strand of hair behind her ear. "Peyton and Jody are coming over in the morning, and we'll have some time then."

"What about your family? There's no privacy when they're around."

"Tomorrow, Hardy. I'll take care of the rest."

His eyes narrowed as he caught something in her voice. "I'm not walking away, Angie. If that's what you think you can convince me to do, then forget it."

She held a hand to her head. "It's not that. Please, I'm getting a tremendous headache. I'll see you tomorrow." She closed the door before he could say another word.

He went down the steps, feeling as if they'd made some progress. In a few days, he had become smitten with his daughter. The connection was strong, and he wanted it to be stronger. But he knew the truth could work against him. Erin may resent him, and he didn't know how he would handle that. It was a risk he had to take because there were no other options. Ten years was too long to be without his child.

THE NEXT MORNING Angie was up early and helped Erin to dress. The whole family showed up before they finished breakfast. They were headed for work and wanted to check in on Erin. She blossomed under their attention.

"I know you're supposed to be on vacation, and we agreed to do the payroll—" AnaMarie placed a plate of tea cakes and kolaches in front of Erin "—but I have a ton of orders to get out by Saturday afternoon, and I need to be in the kitchen. Do you think you could do the payroll?"

Angie hadn't even thought of her job in the past few days. Her only thoughts had been of Erin and Hardy.

"Yeah, sis." Bubba stole a tea cake. "I have to pick up a car in Killeen, and I'm hopeless with numbers."

Angie sighed. "What would y'all do if I was in Florida?"

"Don't worry about my payroll," her dad spoke up. "I can at least write a check, unlike my son and daughter."

With everything crowding in on her, she didn't know how she would get everything done, but it would probably be better to deal with it now instead of trying to straighten out their errors later. "The checks might be late, but I'll have them ready by the afternoon. Just have the hours ready. I don't want to have to chase you down to get those."

"Don't put your sister through any extra stress," Doris said. "She has her hands full taking care of Erin."

"We know." Patsy made a face. "We're not idiots."

Doris let that slide with a small smile at Angie. She cupped Erin's face and kissed her. "I'm so glad my grandbaby's okay. I'm going to the church to help with a fundraiser, so I'll light a candle and say a special prayer for you."

"Thanks, Grandma," Erin mumbled around a mouthful of tea cake.

Angie breathed a sigh of relief as everyone left. But it was only the beginning of the long day. Peyton and Jody soon arrived, and Angie set the girls up in the living room watching movies. The two were whispering and giggling as she and Peyton went into the kitchen.

The TV was turned up loud, so Angie knew the girls couldn't hear them. "I have to tell you something. I'm about to burst."

Peyton poured a cup of coffee and sat at the table. "What is it? You look stressed."

Angie sank into a chair. "You wouldn't believe me."

"Try me."

Angie fiddled with her cup, hating to tell her friend about her past, but if she could tell anyone, she could tell Peyton. "My ex is not Erin's father."

"Mmm." Peyton lifted a finely arched eyebrow. "And Hardy is."

Angie gasped. "How do you know that?"

"Hardy told Wyatt, and we don't keep secrets from each other."

Angie was stunned that Hardy had told someone. "When did Hardy do this?"

"Right after you told him. He got drunk and was parked at the courthouse, drinking straight Jack Daniel's. Wyatt sobered him up, and they talked."

Angie ran her hands over her face, not knowing what to say. At this point she felt like scum at the bottom of a pond.

"Why haven't you ever told me?" Peyton asked.

"I don't know. It's just something not easy to share, and it happened before you came to Horseshoe. And maybe because I wanted you to believe I was that sweet, innocent young girl you thought I was."

"I still do, but I'm finding it a little hard to picture you and Hardy."

"Why?"

"I don't know." Peyton grew thoughtful. "I guess I

see you as a hometown girl with hometown values and Hardy as an uptown man with big dreams. Does that make sense?"

"Yeah." Angie twisted her hands around her coffee cup. She knew exactly what her friend meant. She wasn't Hardy's type. It had been obvious eleven years ago, and it was even more so today.

Peyton took a pinch of an apple kolache and popped it into her mouth. "These things are addictive, and I just got my weight back to what it was before J.W. was born."

"Please." Angie rolled her eyes.

Peyton took another pinch. "Have you ever worked in the kitchen at the bakery?"

"Heavens, no. I worked there since I was about twelve, but the baking is always left to the older ladies with the guarded secret recipe. Grandma Ruby has it in a safe-deposit box."

"Who had the original?"

"My great-great-grandfather married a Czech woman, and she started the bakery many years ago. But, ironically, it's been handed down through the sons. A wife has always taken over the bakery. But now AnaMarie will probably be the first Wiznowski woman to take over."

Peyton picked up the kolache and took a big bite. "Whatever the recipe is, it's delicious." She got up to refill her coffee cup and leaned against the counter. "So how did you and Hardy hook up?"

Angie arched an eyebrow. "I love the way you slipped that in there."

Peyton resumed her seat. "Spill the beans. I'm dying of curiosity."

Angie shrugged. "It's not much to tell. I was a friend of his sister, Rachel. Everyone was Rachel's friend. She was very popular. Then her mother was killed and she became very reclusive and standoffish."

"Wyatt told me about the shooting. How sad."

"It was. Rachel struggled for a long time. Most of her friends just gave up trying to reach her."

"But you hung in there?"

"Yeah. I became her only friend. When summer came, I'd work at the bakery and then go to her house because she kept calling. It was a pattern that summer. Hardy was finishing up law school and was home a lot. He finally moved home from his apartment in Austin, and he was there all the time. We spent most of our time trying to cheer up Rachel. We played games, watched movies and swam in their pool. It was…"

"What?"

"The best time of my life." As she said the words, she realized it had been the summer she'd fallen in love. Hardy had paid attention to her and made her feel special. For a young Angie that had been a big turn-on and… She pushed the thought away. "Rachel was an artist and spent most of her time drawing or painting on an easel. Hardy and I cooked in the kitchen, picked out movies and swam a lot in the pool. I knew I was younger and not his type, but it didn't change the way I started to feel about him. And he…he made me feel beautiful. I never felt like that before."

"Angie, you're the most beautiful person I know."

She glanced at her friend. "On the inside. People tell me that all the time."

"Angie, that's not true."

"Yes, it is. I've never been a raving beauty, but that summer I was beautiful. Every woman needs to feel beautiful at least once in their lifetime."

"Now you're making me sad."

"Don't be. It doesn't bother me that I'm not a knock-out hottie. I'm comfortable with who I am."

"You should be. I've never had a better friend than you and, for the record, I think you're beautiful—on the outside." Peyton slid the rest of the kolache into her mouth. "So the relationship became intimate?"

She told her about the night of the party. "I thought I loved him and nothing else mattered. Not my upbringing. Not my faith. Not my family. Just love like I wanted it to be in my fantasy. Color me naive."

"Do you still love him?"

Angie gave a fake laugh. "I don't know what love is anymore. When I look in Erin's eyes, I see love so pure and innocent. I see the future and happiness. Other than that, I've closed myself off to the yearnings of my heart."

"That's not healthy."

"I know." She brushed a crumb from the table. "Hardy's coming over, and we have to discuss Erin and the future. Do you mind watching the girls while I talk to him in private?"

"Of course not."

"I…I have to tell Erin today, too, and I don't know how I'm going to do that."

Peyton got up and hugged her. "I'll be here if you need anything. Gramma Mae has the little tornado so I'm good for a few hours. Anything you want me to do?"

Angie looked up and tried to smile. "Would you mind telling my family about Hardy?"

Peyton shook her head. "No way in hell. I'm your friend, but I'm not stepping into that maze of total confusion and insanity. Sorry."

"Gee. You said *anything*."

"All I can say is you'd better have a lot of rosary beads around when you tell your mother."

"I don't think there's enough in the world that could open her rigid heart. She might even make me wear a scarlet letter."

Peyton resumed her seat. "Angie Wiznowski, the fallen woman. Oh, my, how will you live that down in this small town?"

"With a lot of prayer."

"Mmm. Everyone in Horseshoe likes you and Erin, and the gossip may fly for a few days, but I believe everyone is going to see this as a love story."

Angie suppressed a laugh. "How much coffee have you had this morning?"

"Enough." Peyton pushed the plate of kolaches away. "What can I say? I'm a romantic."

"I was, too. Once." Angie glanced at the kitchen clock and got to her feet. "I'll call Hardy. It shouldn't take him long to get here. I'll talk with him in the backyard. Just keep Erin occupied."

"No problem. I'm good at keeping kids occupied." Peyton winked. "Please smile or something. It's not the end of the world. I promise."

Angie took her cup to the sink. Peyton saw the world through rose-colored glasses, and Angie was more of a realist. Today just might be the end of her world.

HARDY DRESSED AND headed for the kitchen with a spring in his step. He was going to see his daughter. That filled him with an incredible joy, a joy he'd never thought he would feel. Everything was brighter and clearer, and he couldn't wait to get to Angie's. They still had problems, but he wasn't so angry anymore. There was a little girl who brought sunshine into his hectic life. How could he be angry?

His dad, Mavis and Harvey were in the kitchen. He was hoping to avoid them, but he was caught.

"'Bout time you got up," his dad said. "It's almost eight o'clock. Don't you have to be at the courthouse?"

Hardy poured a cup of coffee. "I've taken a few days off."

"Why? You cleared up everything with hitting that little girl, didn't you?"

"Yes, Dad. I can take care of my own life, thank you."

"Taking a few days off doesn't sound like you're taking care of business. It seems personal, and personal will always get you in trouble. You have to keep your eye on Judge Wexler's seat. The man has to be replaced at next year's election. He's too lenient with criminals. I don't know how many times I have to tell you this."

Hardy took a sip of coffee to calm himself. "Let's make this the last time, then, because I'm tired of hearing it."

"Don't get smart with me. I'm thinking of your future."

Hardy stared directly at his father. "Why? I'm thirty-four years old, and I can handle my future. Alone, without any help or pressure from you. I love you, Dad, but please give me my space."

Hardison threw up his hands. "Fine. Have you talked to Olivia this morning?"

"No, but we spoke last night. She's busy with a trial, and I'll see her this weekend." He had to find a way to tell Olivia about Erin. She wasn't going to be pleased, but he hoped at least she'd be happy for him. They'd had their ups and downs over the past year and a ten-year-old child was not in their plans. She'd adjust, as he was.

"I don't know about this long-distance relationship, but I know Olivia is good for you and your career." The judge got to his feet. "I'm going into Austin for a day or two. I'll stay at the club. Hector and Palo have gone to Mexico to visit family, and Harvey could probably use your help around the ranch."

"Now, Judge, I don't need any help," Harvey said.

His father had a one-track mind, and everything had to be done his way. Hardy had dealt with that attitude since he was a kid. Maybe it was time for him to find his own place. He'd certainly want to make a home for Erin so he could spend some time with her.

Going to a club was his dad's way of saying he was seeing his lady friend. But to be fair, he did belong to a private men's club and he spent a lot of time there playing golf and cards. It was his way of dealing with stress.

"Sorry, Dad, but I have other plans today."

"Like what?"

"I plan to spend some time with Erin."

His dad frowned. "Who's Erin?"

My daughter, he wanted to say. But instead he said, "The little girl I hit."

"Haven't you done enough damage control there?"

"Not nearly enough." He headed for the door. "I'll catch you later."

"Don't you want breakfast?" Mavis called.

"Thanks. I'm good."

In minutes he was on his way to Angie's. This could be the day. No. This *had* to be the day Angie told Erin about him. He had to be prepared for Erin's reaction.

ANGIE PACED IN the backyard. A privacy fence enclosed it, and it was the only place they wouldn't be disturbed. The fence had been a big selling point to the house. Erin would have a big yard to play in. The large oaks were another plus.

The cowbells, petunias and zinnias were in bloom. The Knock Out Roses against the fence were about to burst forth with color. She had worked for weeks so the yard would be perfect for Erin's birthday. The shrubs were trimmed and not a weed dared to poke its head up in her flower beds.

The trampoline had been Erin's birthday gift last year. The swing set Erin had gotten when she was five. Bubba had also hung a rope swing on a branch of a big oak. Angie had added the barbecue pit, picnic table and chairs to the patio soon after she'd bought the house. It was all familiar to her, and it would be easier to talk in this surrounding.

The side gate opened, and Hardy walked toward her. The concern on his handsome face was a warning this wasn't going to be an easy conversation. He wore jeans, boots and a long-sleeved white shirt. He had an easy way of moving that denoted strength and confidence. His lean body was well toned from exercise. She often saw him running around Horseshoe before he started his day.

It was the beginning of June, and the weather was getting warmer. A natural heat bathed her face. She wanted to look away from him, but she had to admit she was as attracted to him as she'd always been. But now she could control her feelings and not dream stupid dreams.

"How's Erin?" he asked.

"She's fine. She's watching movies with Jody."

"I saw Peyton's Suburban out front." He stepped onto the patio and sat at the redwood table. "If you're planning to talk me out of telling Erin, you're wasting your time."

She took a seat across from him because her legs were shaky. "I'd like to know your plans concerning Erin."

He frowned. "What do you mean?"

"You have a girlfriend. I'd like to know how Erin will fit into your life. Erin's happiness is my main concern."

"To tell you the truth, I haven't had time to think about it."

"Have you told Olivia? I believe that's her name."

He rubbed his hand across the surface of the table. "No."

"Why not?"

"This has hit me out of the blue, and I'm more focused on forming a connection to my daughter than anything else."

She had to say the words she hadn't said the night she'd told him. She took a deep breath. "I apologize for never telling you about Erin. I know it doesn't mean much now, but at the time I did the best that I could."

He shifted uneasily in the chair. She would've sworn he would never apologize, but he said, "And I apologize for not getting in touch after that night."

His sincere words opened a floodgate of questions. "Why didn't you? Why wouldn't you call to see how I was? Maybe you've had a lot of nights like that. I'm sorry if I sound naive, but we had a fun summer and I couldn't imagine why you would just suddenly push me out of your life. I never expected anything from you."

Her eyes never wavered from his. All she wanted was an honest answer.

He looked off to the oak tree shading the swing set. "It was a summer I'll never forget for more than one reason. Rachel and I were both struggling with our mother's sudden death. You helped us to talk about her, and the more we talked, the more the pain lessened. I was grateful to you for so many things."

"Please don't tell me it was gratitude sex, because I'm

not going to believe that on any day of the week. I'm not that naive."

He threw up his hands. "What do you want from me, Angie?"

"I want you to be honest."

He stood up, brimming with restless energy. "I have a lot going on in my life at the moment. I'm planning to run for my dad's old judge seat. Olivia is handling getting my name out to the voters. I'll be attending a lot of meetings, dinners and rallies, but I still want to be part of my daughter's life. I intend to be part of my daughter's life."

"I want to make this clear—for now Erin stays here. I don't want Erin thrown into a political campaign, and I don't want her thrown into a tug-of-war between us. This is her home, and until she adjusts to having a father, that's the way it will be."

"You don't get to make the rules, Angie."

She got to her feet, new energy surging through her. When it came to Erin, she would fight him tooth and nail. "I make the rules concerning my daughter. Get used to it, Hardy, because that's the way it's going to be."

His eyes darkened. "I could fight you for custody."

She stared him straight in the eye. "Really? You care so much for your daughter that you would put her through that?"

"You're making me say things I don't mean. I would never hurt Erin."

"But you would love to hurt me, wouldn't you?"

His angry eyes caught hers. "I still don't understand why you couldn't have found some way to get in touch with me."

"And I don't understand why you couldn't have taken five minutes to talk to me or even call after that summer.

You made me feel like an inconvenience you wanted to forget."

"It wasn't that, and you know it."

"No, I don't, because you're not being honest. Did you think I wanted something from you? Like renewing our relationship?" The flash of guilt in his eyes said it all. "It was."

He looked at her then. "Yes. That summer was also a painful time as I put the memories of my mother to rest. Every time I saw you, I thought I didn't want to go back there. I didn't want to relive that. I'd just rather go on with my life."

She'd wanted him to be honest, and, oh, he was honest with a vengeance. She wanted to ignore the pain in her heart, but she hadn't matured that much. It hurt like hell to be told she was nothing but a painful memory. Okay, she could handle this. She'd handled so much more.

"Thank you for being honest." The words tasted like sawdust in her mouth.

"I'm sorry if that hurts."

"Sure you are." She hated she couldn't keep the sarcasm out of her voice. "Let's get back to what's important. Erin."

"I want you to tell her today."

She started to object but knew she would only be doing so out of spite. She wouldn't do that to Erin. Her daughter needed to know the truth. Damn, honesty was going to kill her.

She held up one finger. "First, you will see Erin here at her home. Second, you will gradually introduce her to your family at your discretion. As I pointed out earlier, I will not have her involved in a political campaign to further your career. She's a little girl who only wants to know her father."

"Agreed."

"I will tell her sometime today when I feel the time is right. If I feel the first resistance that she's not receptive, I will not tell her. The time has to be right."

"Okay. We have a deal." He held out his hand. She glanced at it and resisted the impulse to ignore him. That would make her look foolish, so she put her hand in his. His big hand clasped hers and memories swelled around her in bits and pieces like a beautiful forgotten song. He was always gentle, caring, and the strength of his hand made her very aware of that. She quickly pulled hers away.

"I hope we can still be friends," he had the nerve to say.

She stared at him. "We've never been friends, not in the way that I count true friendship."

He shrugged. "Angie, there doesn't need to be tension between us."

"There won't be as long as you don't hurt Erin. That's my bottom line." She turned and walked into the house with part of her pride intact. The rest of her pride had been shredded like newspaper for confetti. Tonight, when she was alone, she would shed tears over a romance that had only existed in a young girl's head.

Chapter Seven

Before Angie turned away, Hardy saw the hurt in her eyes. At the sight, all the anger swooshed from him like air from a balloon. He tried to understand why he'd hurt her. It wasn't intentional, but it sure felt like it.

PEYTON LEFT TO pick up J.W. and Jody stayed with Erin. They were engrossed in a movie. Angie sat at the kitchen table, and her mind went back to that night long ago.

She'd never had any kind of liquor or beer, and the spiked punch had had her reeling. Hardy was like her knight in shining armor coming to rescue her. He'd helped her into his bed and she'd wrapped his sheet around her and rested her head on his pillow. That manly, soapy scent she associated with him was all around her, and she'd drifted into blissful sleep.

When she'd awoken, he had been there and it had been like a dream come true. She'd been in love with him for so long, and it seemed natural to kiss him because in her heart she knew he felt the same way about her. The kiss was the most sensual experience of her life. She hadn't thought; she'd just gone with her feelings. Touching his skin, his shoulders, his chest until they were skin on skin and the world was forgotten. It was only them in that moment.

It had been her first time. When she'd felt the pain, he had tried to draw away, but she wouldn't let him. After that, there had been no turning back. It was an experience she would never forget because she'd given Hardy a part of herself that morning and he had given her the most precious gift of all: Erin.

Everything had been just like she'd dreamed. Hardy was all she'd ever wanted. Then he had moved from the bed, leaving her alone and vulnerable. She'd scooted up in bed, holding the sheet around her bare breasts and watching his troubled face.

"I'm sorry, Angie," he'd said. "This should never have happened. God, I'm so sorry."

"What for? I wanted it, too."

"You're so young you don't know what you want." She hadn't missed the note of regret in his voice.

"I may be young, but I know how I feel about you."

He'd rammed his hands through his disheveled hair. "Please don't say you love me."

"I do."

He had shaken his head vigorously. "No, you don't. It's just a crush. That's all, and I took advantage of it. I knew how you felt about me, and I should never have touched you."

She'd bitten her lip to keep from crying. Everything she had believed about love had just been destroyed. She wasn't someone special. She was just another girl to him. She'd wanted to hang her head and run until she couldn't feel the pain anymore. Instead, she had crawled from the bed, grabbed her clothes and slipped into them as quickly as she could.

Her hands had shaken while her stomach heaved.

"Angie, please, I'm not trying to hurt you."

"Doesn't matter," she'd mumbled, slipping into her sandals.

"This was a mistake. Can't you see that?"

She'd stood up straight and stared at him with more courage than she'd been feeling. "I'm sorry I'm not up on the proper etiquette for affairs or one-night stands." Gathering every ounce of her pride, she had marched out of the room and left behind both the man she'd loved with all her heart...and her girlhood.

With a sigh, Angie got up and went into the living room. Peyton and J.W. came back, and Peyton agreed to stay so Angie could run to her office to do payroll. The girls were laughing at J.W.'s antics as Angie went toward the door.

"Stay put," she said to Erin. "I'll be back in a few minutes."

"Aw, Mama. I'm not a baby."

"But you're injured, and I expect you to be on the sofa when I return."

"Yes, ma'am."

It didn't take long, and she was back within thirty minutes. She waved goodbye to Peyton and the kids as they drove away and then walked back into the house. It was time, and Angie struggled to find the right words. How do you tell a child you've lied to her for years? By being as honest as possible now.

Erin sat on the sofa, propped up on pillows with her legs outstretched in front of her. She had iPod earbuds in her ears and was singing Katy Perry's "Roar." Angie sat on the coffee table facing her.

Erin removed the earbuds. "When is Mr. Hardy coming? He's usually here by this time."

The perfect opening. Angie carefully chose her words. "You like Mr. Hardy?"

"Yeah. He's cool. Mama, Jody and I watched a scary movie. You might have to sleep with me so I won't be freaked out." Erin's attention span jumped around like the ten-year-old she was.

"I didn't get you any scary movies."

"We watched it on TV."

"Did Peyton know you were watching it?"

Erin shrugged and looked guilty.

"You switched the channel when I left, didn't you?"

Erin played with a bud of her iPod she had in her lap and didn't answer.

"You know I don't like you watching those movies. It's hard for you to sleep."

"I have a big mouth."

"But I love you."

"Aw, Mama." She looked up with an impish grin. "It would be real hard to punish me 'cause I'm hurt, right?"

"Right." She tried not to smile.

"Can we have pizza for lunch? You know, the kind you make with cheese and pepperoni that's so-o good."

Angie glanced at the clock on the wall. "It's almost noon. How about if we have the pizza for supper and something simple for lunch?"

"Okay."

"I'd like to talk about something first."

"What?"

Angie took a deep breath. "You've asked me several times about your father."

Erin sat up straight. "He heard about my accident and he's coming to see me?"

Angie shook her head at Erin's excitement. "No, sweetie."

Erin sank back, disappointed. "Then what?"

Angie searched for words, but none were there. She

had to go with what was on her mind. "I'd like to talk about him."

That got Erin's attention. She sat up again. "I know his name is Dennis Green and Grandma said he was a loser and we were better off without him and I wasn't to ask any more questions."

Angie was horrified. She had no idea her mother had told Erin this. That was Angie's fault, though. She should have been more open with her daughter.

She took another deep breath. "I have to tell you some things, and it's not going to be easy, but I hope you will listen with an open heart because above all else I love you."

"Jeez, Mama, you scaring me more than the movie."

This was it. She had to say the words. "Dennis Green is not your biological father."

Erin's eyes grew huge, and it was obvious she didn't understand. "But you married him. He has to be my father."

So simple in a child's mind.

"I made a lot of bad choices when I was young. I fell in love with a man who was older and I thought I loved him. In my heart I did."

Erin just stared at her. Angie forced herself to continue. "He left town soon afterward. When I found out I was pregnant, I couldn't get in touch with him. I was scared and didn't know what to do. Then I met Dennis, and we were very good friends. We decided to get married because I couldn't face your grandmother. I guess I was a coward because that was one of the worst decisions I ever made."

"Grandma would have had a cow."

That was putting it mildly. "Yes, but it wasn't fair to Dennis for me to marry him when I didn't love him."

"So you got a divorce?"

"Yes, baby." The marriage was later annulled, but Erin didn't need to know that right now.

"My daddy left and never came back and he never asked about me?"

"He never knew about you."

"You should have told him, Mama. Maybe he wanted us."

All those protective walls Angie had built around herself were beginning to shake and crumble, and she didn't know if she could continue.

She swallowed something that felt like a Brillo pad. "He finally came back to Horseshoe, and I didn't know how to tell him that he had a daughter."

"It's okay, Mama. He probably didn't want us anyway." Erin saw the sadness on Angie's face and she was trying to make it better. That was her daughter. She had a loving spirit.

Angie blew out a breath. "Fate took it out of my hands, sweetie, and I had to tell him."

Her eyes grew big once again. "He knows about me?"

"Yes."

"Is he coming to see me?"

"You've already seen him—many times."

"I have? Who is he?"

Angie drew a scorching breath and knew she had no choice but to answer. "Your…your biological father is Hardison Hollister."

Erin's mouth formed a big O, and she couldn't speak for a moment. "Mr. Hardy is my father? My real father?"

"Yes, baby."

The O was replaced with a big frown. "Mr. Hardy has been in Horseshoe for a long time. Why did you never tell me? Why did you never tell me I had a father?" The frown deepened. "You said we should never lie, and you lied to me. I've seen him over at Jody's. One time I fell and scraped my knee and he carried me inside. My father carried me, and I didn't even know it. How could you keep that secret from me? I'm not a baby. I hate you." Erin struggled to her feet. Angie trembled, but she knew not to touch Erin now. She was angry, and she had a right to be. Erin grabbed her crutches. "I don't want you to be my mother anymore. Real mothers don't lie." Fat tears ran down her cheeks. Angie felt sick to her stomach as Erin hobbled to her room. Angie slowly followed.

Erin plopped onto her bed; the crutches fell to the floor.

Angie picked them up and placed them against the wall. "I'm sorry, baby."

"No, you're not," Erin shouted. "Mr. Hardy is a nice man and he would've wanted me, but you—"

"Erin—"

"I want to go live with Jody."

Angie fought to breathe. "Sorry, that's not going to happen. I'm your mother, and you belong with me."

"I'm old enough to know," Erin shouted again.

"Yes, you are. I failed you. I'm sorry."

Angie didn't have any strength left. She walked out of the room and sat at the kitchen table. Where did she go from here? If she lost her daughter, she would lose everything. That was when the tears came. She cried for all the mistakes she'd made. She cried for hurting the one person she loved most in this world. And she cried for the young girl who'd been so young and foolish.

Chapter Eight

After leaving Angie's, Hardy went to the courthouse to check his schedule and his messages. He didn't have court until Monday, so his weekend was free to spend with his daughter. He checked his phone several times, but Angie hadn't called. It was hard not to call her, but he would be patient. Telling Erin would be tough for Angie; he understood that.

He spoke to his secretary, Alice, and there was nothing that needed his immediate attention. As he left his office, he ran into Wyatt.

"How's it going?" Wyatt asked.

Hardy glanced at his watch. "Angie's telling Erin I'm her father."

"You want to go get a cup of coffee and talk?"

"Nah. I'm waiting for the call, and then I'm going to see my daughter. This time it will be as her father."

Wyatt slapped him on the shoulder. "I'm glad. Erin will adjust quickly. She's just as sweet as her mother."

Hardy already knew that. Erin was a clone of Angie: her mannerisms, her smile, her personality. She had the ability to charm people just with her presence. Of course, he might be prejudiced.

"I filled out a report on the accident," Wyatt said. "For

the record. I know you don't want anything to come back and bite you in the butt when you run for office."

The election was the furthest thing from his mind. All that mattered was his daughter. The thought surprised him. For years all that had mattered was his career.

"Hardy Hollister, how could you run over that sweet child?" Mrs. Satterwhite walked up to them, clearly armed with gossip and ready to defend Erin.

"I didn't do it on purpose," he replied. "It was an accident."

"You weren't paying attention." She shook a finger at him. "You were probably on your phone like all young folks."

"No, ma'am, I wasn't. Erin came out of nowhere before I could stop."

"That's true, Mrs. Satterwhite," Wyatt spoke up. "I saw the whole thing. I was there. Erin was playing with a ball, and it bounced into the street. She ran after it without thinking. Hardy turned the corner about the same time, and there was no way to prevent what happened. It was an accident."

Mrs. Satterwhite pushed her purse farther up her arm. "If you say so, Sheriff. That poor baby. Angie must be beside herself."

"Yes, she is," Hardy said. "I'm making sure Erin has everything she needs, and she will be better soon."

Mrs. Satterwhite touched his arm. "You should. Your father would want you to."

Hardy gritted his teeth and kept his response to himself.

"Good seeing you, Mrs. Satterwhite." Wyatt tipped his hat as the woman walked off. Wyatt glanced at him. "Get used to that attitude."

"I could care less what the old biddies of this town

think." He looked at his watch again. "I don't understand why Angie hasn't called. I think I might go over there and check."

"Don't push it, Hardy. Peyton and Jody were at Angie's most of the morning. Angie probably hasn't had time to tackle such a sensitive subject. Just be patient."

"See you later." Hardy ignored the advice because his very life depended on what was happening at Angie's house.

Hardy drove around to the garage. Angie's SUV was inside, so he got out and walked to the back door. After tapping lightly, he waited. There was no answer. He opened it slightly.

"Angie," he murmured, not wanting to speak too loud in case she was with Erin. Still no response. Against his better judgment, he walked into the kitchen, then stopped short.

Angie was pounding some dough on the kitchen table. Flour was all over the table, Angie and the floor. She kept striking it with her fist. He assumed she was supposed to be kneading it.

"Angie, what are you doing?"

She looked up, wiped a tear away and smeared flour across her cheek. "Making Erin a pizza. She wants pizza and…"

Seeing she was about to fall apart, he caught her arms and guided her backward to a chair. "What happened?"

"She hates me. She doesn't want me to be her mother anymore because I lied to her all these years." She wiped more tears away with her floury hand and made white trails on her face.

He squatted in front of her. "She's just hurt. She didn't mean it."

Angie hiccuped. "I didn't think she would take it this

hard. She has a loving spirit and a good heart. We've always had a good relationship. Now...I'm a mother who lied and she's never going to forgive me."

He glanced at the hammered dough. "But you're making her pizza, so she must've asked for it."

Angie hiccuped again. "She asked for it before I told her." She got up and grabbed a napkin off the counter and wiped her nose. "I did what you wanted. Now could you please leave us alone so we can have some privacy?"

He stood, thinking about his options, thinking about her hurt feelings. He didn't see any other way. "No. As I see it, we're in this together—as parents. May I talk to her, please?"

She glared at him. "Why? So you can tell her what an awful person I am? I've had enough for one day, Hardy."

"Do you really think I would do that?"

She flung out a hand. "I don't know. I don't know anything anymore. All I know is I'm losing my child."

"She's ten years old, and she's hurt. We just have to give her time."

"And you're an expert now?"

He clamped his mouth shut and took a moment. "The two of us bickering is not helping matters."

She blew her nose into the napkin. "Fine. Go talk to her, but if she wants you to leave, I want you to go. We all need some time."

He stared into her troubled eyes. "You really wish I would just go away, don't you?"

Glancing away to some childish drawings on the refrigerator, she replied, "I wish I could go back and change things. I wish I had been stronger and not cared what my mother thought or what anyone thought. I wish so many things, but one thing I don't wish is for Erin to be without her father any longer."

"Thank you." Without knowing what else to say, he turned toward the hall.

His feet felt as if they had been encased in cement as he walked toward his daughter's room. He wasn't known to be a praying man, but a lot of prayers shot through his head as he tapped on the door and waited for his daughter to respond.

ANGIE REACHED FOR a dish towel and rinsed it under the faucet and then wiped her face. She was a mess, and she had to regain control. Erin would come around, she kept telling herself. But when Angie remembered the hurt in her child's eyes, she hated herself for what she'd done to someone she loved with all her heart.

Mistakes and regrets were knocking on her door like avenging angels seeking revenge. The next few hours would define her future, and she didn't know if she had the strength to face it. But she had to, as she had years ago. This time she hoped she made better decisions.

Unable to stop herself, she tiptoed down the hall to see what was happening. Yes, it was wrong. At this point, though, she didn't care. She just wanted her daughter to be happy again.

"I guess your mom told you," Hardy was saying.

"That you're my dad? Yes." Erin's voice was still defiant, and Angie's stomach cramped.

"How do you feel about that?"

"I'm mad at my mama, and I'm mad at you, too."

"You have a right to be angry."

"Good, because I am."

"Do you mind if I sit down?"

"I don't care."

The only chair in Erin's room was her desk chair, and Angie heard it as it dragged across the hardwood floor.

"I like your room, pink and white and bright. Are the drawings on the wall yours?"

"Yes. Mama had them framed. She thought they were good."

"My sister is an artist, and she lives in New York."

"Really?"

"Yes, really. I think she would like you."

There was silence for a moment. Angie wanted to creep away, but she couldn't make herself move.

"You know, sometimes adults make mistakes." Hardy's voice was soft yet strong. "Your mother and I made a big mistake, and all we can do now is try to make it better."

"Why didn't you call my mother? Why did you leave her and not come back?"

The silence scraped along Angie's nerve endings.

"I'm not real sure. I had a new job and new responsibilities. I moved on with my life. Your mom did, too."

"That's just an excuse. My mama is the best. I don't want to talk to you anymore."

Angie heard a movement, and she knew Hardy had gotten to his feet.

"I hope in the days ahead you'll find it in your heart to forgive me. If not, please forgive your mother. It's breaking her heart that you're hurting and it's breaking mine, too. She loves you more than life itself. Maybe one day you will give me a chance to love you, too."

Angie hurried back to the kitchen, wiping away more tears. She picked up the ruined dough and tossed it in the garbage. She had literally beaten the life out of it, and she had to start over.

Hardy stood in the doorway, pale and a little shaky. "I've known pain before, but nothing like this."

With a dish towel, she wiped some flour off the table, trying not to look at the hurt on his face.

"I'll check back later," he said, heading for the door.

"Mama. I want my mama!" Erin screeched.

Angie dropped the towel and ran toward Erin's room. Nothing mattered but her daughter.

HARDY STOOD IN the middle of the kitchen, unsure of what to do. Sucking air into his tight lungs, he quickly followed Angie.

She sat on the bed, holding Erin while their daughter sobbed into her chest. Neither acknowledged his presence.

"I'm sorry. I don't hate you. I don't want anyone else for my mama. I love you."

Angie stroked Erin's hair. "Shh. It's okay. Stop crying." But the crying didn't stop, and Hardy's chest contracted at the pitiful sobs. Finally, the sobs turned to hiccups.

Angie held Erin's face and kissed her cheek. "You okay?"

Erin wrapped her arms around her mother's waist. "Don't let me go."

"I'm not. I'm your mother and I'll always be here."

After a moment, Erin calmed down and drew back. "Is Mr. Hardy really my father?"

"Yes, baby, he is. I'm sorry it took me so long to tell you."

Erin shrugged. "Well, I've always wanted a father, and now I have one."

"We can take this slow." Angie glanced at him and he nodded, glad she was including him. "We don't have to rush into anything. I'm sure Hardy will agree."

"Yes," he replied, even though he knew his answer wasn't required.

"It's okay, Mama. I'm not a baby. I just don't understand why you couldn't tell me."

Angie pulled her daughter close. "I don't either, sweetheart. There never seemed to be a right time. And then there's your grandmother. I wasn't sure how to explain my behavior to her. I'm a coward."

Erin giggled, and it was a precious sound. "Oh, Mama, how are we going to tell Grandma? She's going to freak out."

"Are you ready for everyone to know?"

Erin looked over her mother's shoulder and stared at him. He was spellbound by his daughter's courage. "I'm not mad at you anymore, Mr. Hardy."

The "Mr. Hardy" part stung, but he wasn't quibbling over that. It would take time for her to call him Daddy. "Thank you, peanut."

"Mama and I are good," Erin said. "I love my mama."

He wanted to ask how she felt about him, but it wasn't the time. "I'm glad."

Angie glanced at him. "I was just asking Erin how she felt about everyone knowing."

Hardy shoved his hands into the pockets of his jeans because they were shaking. "And?"

Erin looked from one to the other. "I want people to know that Mr. Hardy is my father. If they don't like it, then they don't have to like me."

His shaking hands stilled, and a smile threatened his lips. He had one hell of a daughter.

Angie got to her feet. "First, I'll have to tell my family. We can do that tonight, if that's okay?"

"We're going to have fireworks, Mama." Erin raised her arms in the air. "And it's not even the Fourth of July."

Erin scooted to the edge of the bed, and Angie braced her. "Baby, be careful with your leg."

"I am." Erin gave her mother the once-over. "You have flour all over you, and now it's on me."

Angie kissed the tip of Erin's nose. "I was trying to make you a pizza and instead gave myself a flour bath."

"Oh, boy. We're going to have Mama's pizza. It's the best." She eyed her mother. "Can Mr. Hardy stay?"

"Sure."

Hardy's tired heart lifted. He loved his daughter more than words could say. As he watched Angie help Erin with her crutches, he knew a lot of his old feelings still lingered for Angie, and that was opening a door that needed to stay closed. He had run from their relationship years ago. Maybe it was time to stand up and be a man. Maybe it was time to stand up and be a father like he should've been when Erin was born.

THE AFTERNOON PASSED quickly as Erin and Hardy chatted and she worked on the pizza. From time to time they offered their advice and nibbled on the cheese and pepperoni. Most of the time the two of them were playing games on his phone. They laughed and joked as if they had been father and daughter from the start. It was a joy to watch them. But it was a lull before the storm.

Twice he was interrupted with phone calls that he took in another room. She assumed they were from Olivia, and she wondered if he'd told Olivia about Erin yet. They would discuss that later.

She called her family and asked that they all come to the house at seven o'clock. She and Erin had something to tell them. Hardy's name wasn't mentioned. She thought it was best for that to be revealed in person.

They ate the pizza at the kitchen table, and Erin talked

nonstop. Most of the time around a mouthful of food. Angie had to stop her several times. Erin didn't normally do that, and Angie could see how excited she was to have Hardy there.

"Didn't I tell you how good Mama's pizza is?"

"I've had your mother's pizza before." Hardy's eyes met hers. A tingle ran through her as she remembered all the times they'd laughed and eaten pizza at the kitchen counter at the Hollister ranch.

Erin's eyes widened. "Really?"

"Your mother used to come to the ranch to visit my sister, Rachel, and Rachel was… How do I say this?" His eyes narrowed in thought, and Angie couldn't drag her gaze away. "Lazy. Yeah, that's it. She'd talk Angie into doing all kinds of things, and making pizza was always at the top of her list."

His eyes continued to hold hers. For a moment they were back in a fun-filled day at the ranch with no responsibilities. No obligations. Just enjoying each other. It seemed like a lifetime ago. It *was* a lifetime ago.

"Oh, no." Erin's hands framed her face in shock. "If you're my father, that means the judge is my grandfather. He's, like, scary."

Hardy looked amused. "Yes, you have another grandfather, but I haven't told him yet." He winked at Erin. "Once you get to know him, he won't be so scary. And he's going to love you."

Erin leaned back in her chair. "Gosh. I have another grandfather and another aunt."

Angie got to her feet. "I'm sure you'll adjust. It's getting close to seven, so we'd better clean up the kitchen before the family descends on us. Sweetie, it might be best if you watched a movie in your room." She wanted to protect Erin from any nasty things that might be said.

"No, Mama. I have to be there. It concerns me. Please." Angie glanced at Hardy. "What do you think?"

His forehead wrinkled in confusion. Obviously, he wasn't expecting her to ask for his opinion. "It will probably be easier for your mother to take if Erin is there. She'll be less likely to make a scene."

"Grandma throws big fits." Erin made a face. "But she loves me, and I want her to meet my daddy."

"Okay." Angie gave in. She didn't want to keep anything from Erin again. She was ten years old—old enough to introduce her father to the family.

"It's going to be showtime, Mr. Hardy," Erin said, drinking the last of her milk. "Don't worry. Grandma's not too bad."

That's an understatement, Angie thought as she wiped the counter and prepared herself for the stressful evening.

Her mother stomped through the front door, her purse over her arm, a frown on her face. "Why do we have to come over here at seven o'clock? It's late, and your father likes to watch TV. I need to clean the kitchen and put my feet up. What's so mysterious that we have to rush over here? I wanted to come by when I finished at the church to see Erin, but you said no. You make life very difficult sometimes, Angie."

Grandma Ruby, her dad's mom, followed them in. She lived next door to Angie's parents and had run the bakery for years. She continued to help out when things got busy. In her seventies, she wasn't keen on working too much. Ruby's mother-in-law, Grandma Helen Wiznowski, lived with her and was still spry at ninety-two, just a little forgetful. Five generations of Wiznowskis still lived in Horseshoe.

Angie knew Grandma Helen wouldn't come. She went to bed at seven o'clock and never left the house after dark.

"I'll make this quick, then," Angie said.

Her father clicked on the TV, and Bubba sat beside him as they flipped through the channels. She took the control out of Bubba's hand. "Sorry, but I need everyone's attention."

Erin and Hardy came in from the kitchen to the living room. Doris gaped at Hardy. "What's he doing here?"

Hardy brought a chair for Erin, held her crutches and made sure she was comfortable. He made no effort to answer Doris. The silence held until Patsy and Peggy came through the door, squabbling.

"He's my customer!" Peggy was almost screaming. "I always cut his hair, but today you had to horn in."

"You were busy with Mrs. Hornsby and he wanted his hair cut," Patsy shot back. "So I cut it. What's the big deal?"

"Screw you."

"Could you not do this now?" Angie asked and wondered, not for the first time, why she cared what her family thought.

AnaMarie rushed through the door. "Sorry I'm late, but there's always a straggler who wants kolaches." She sat next to her mother on the sofa. Grandma Ruby took the big chair.

Patsy jumped up and hugged Erin. "I haven't seen my sweetie all day, and I need a hug." Her eyes settled on Hardy. "Hey, dark knight, still hanging around, huh? Guilt's a bitch."

"Watch your language," Doris scolded.

"Yes, ma'am." Patsy rolled her eyes and went back to her chair.

All eyes turned to Angie. She wasn't sure how to start the conversation, but she was sure she wanted to get it over with as soon as possible.

"Sis," Bubba chimed in. "Say what you have to say because I have to get back to the gas station."

"Okay." She held up both hands. "Since everyone is in a hurry, I'll make this brief." She had the urge to glance at Hardy, but she didn't. Her lungs felt tight, and she forced the words through an equally tight throat. "Dennis Green is not Erin's father."

Golden silence followed her announcement; the only sound was the water sprinkler next door hitting the house when it made the circle.

"Don't be absurd, Angie," her mother said. "And why would you bring this up with Erin in the room? This isn't something she needs to hear."

"I already know, Grandma," Erin surprised Angie by answering her grandmother.

Doris gasped. "What's going on, Angie? And why is Mr. Hollister here? This is family, and he's not included."

She faced her mother, saying words she should've said ten years ago. "He's here because he's Erin's biological father."

Chapter Nine

"What?" Her mother's mouth fell open, and everyone else was too stunned to speak. Doris regained her composure quickly. "Are you saying you slept with this man?" She pointed to Hardy.

"Yes," she replied without pausing. Without blinking. Without squirming.

"How could you? You were raised better than that. My daughters do not sleep around. He must've taken advantage of you."

"He did not take advantage of me. I'd been in love with him for a long time."

"That's why you spent so much time at the Hollister ranch. It wasn't to see Rachel. It was to see *him*."

The conversation was between Angie and her mother. Everyone else listened closely. She never wavered as she answered, "Yes. I was crazy about him. We spent a lot of time together. I knew he was older, and it didn't seem to matter. At Rachel's going-away party someone spiked the punch and I got a little tipsy."

Her mother made the sign of the cross, clasped her hands and began to pray silently with her head bent.

Angie refused to stop. Doris had to hear the whole story. "I couldn't come home because I knew you would throw a fit so Hardy let me spend the night. The next morning we got carried away. Later, we both agreed it was a mistake. He left for Europe, and I went to junior college in Temple. I soon discovered I was pregnant, and I couldn't get in touch with him. I didn't know what I was going to do. I had classes with Dennis, and we were good friends. When he offered to marry me, I jumped at the chance because I couldn't come home and face you. I knew you would condemn, judge and berate me, and I just didn't want to go through that. So I had my baby alone. It wasn't until after Erin was born that I called Patsy and Peggy because I could no longer hold it together. Go ahead and say what you need to say because it's not going to change a thing."

Doris raised her head and glared. "You are such a disappointment, Angie. How could you disgrace me like this?"

Angie's heart sank at the bitter words, but she did not bend under the criticism. Too much was at stake.

"Mrs. Wiznowski, I'm sorry you're upset," Hardy joined in. "But like Angie said, it's not going to change a thing. Blame me if it makes you feel better."

"You better believe I blame you. Judge Hollister will hear about this."

"My father has nothing to do with what happened."

"You took advantage of Angie and her trusting nature."

"He did not," Angie quickly denied.

"It doesn't matter," Hardy said. "Angie was eighteen, and I was well over twenty-one. We were adults and free to do what we wanted. If that's hard for you to understand, then I'm sorry for you. This meeting was a courtesy to the family. We didn't want you to find out some other way, but maybe sometimes you just can't be nice to certain people."

"How dare you!" Doris spat.

Bubba got to his feet. "I'm gonna kill him like I should have days ago."

"Sit down, son," Willard said, his voice strong like it was when he was serious. "This is none of your concern. Nor ours, either. This is Angie's life, and she's made decisions that I regret, but they were hers to make. I regret them because she didn't feel she could come to us when she was in trouble. That hurts. I understand the reasoning, though." He looked at his wife. "What kind of mother drives her daughter away?"

"Shut up, Willard. I raised our girls to be religious, moral women. I did not raise them to be sluts and sleep around and hide it and have children out of wedlock. That's a sin against God."

"Really?" Grandma Ruby piped up. "You didn't remember that when you were sleeping with Willard before you were married."

"Mama!" her dad scolded.

Everyone else in the room gasped, and Doris looked as if she'd been slapped.

But it seemed her grandmother wasn't through. "You need to practice what you preach, Doris."

Willard got to his feet, walked over to Angie and hugged her. She choked back tears. "I'm sorry I wasn't there for you. Now I'm going home and let you handle your life and Erin's because I love you." On his way to the door he hugged Erin, reached in his pocket and gave her a quarter. He always did that. Erin had a piggy bank full of quarters.

He shook Hardy's hand. "Welcome to the family."

"Thank you, sir," Hardy replied. "I appreciate your understanding, especially during this difficult time."

Willard looked at his wife. "Are you coming?"

"I'd rather walk than ride with your mother." Her stormy eyes indicated a heated conversation was coming concerning Grandma Ruby.

"Suit yourself. Bubba, it's time for you to go, too. It's time for everyone to go. C'mon, Mama. We need to talk, too."

Grandma Ruby eased from her chair and approached Angie. Hugging her, she said, "Bless you, child. Never be afraid to stand up for yourself." Then she whispered under her breath, "Don't worry about your mom. She's a lot of hot air." She pinched Erin's cheek and followed her son.

Bubba gave Hardy the stink eye before he went out the door. An awkward silence filled the room after they left.

"Well, well, well, isn't this something?" Patsy got up. "You just walked away and left Angie pregnant?"

"Drop it, Patsy. This conversation is over, and I do not need anyone to protect me from Hardy. I'm the one who didn't tell him about Erin, so all of this is on me. Erin has forgiven me. That's all that matters."

Doris finally got to her feet, her purse clutched tightly in her arms. "I will never forgive you for the disgrace you have brought to this family."

Angie held her ground. "That's your prerogative."

"Disgrace, Mrs. Wiznowski?" Hardy's voice was cold and sharp, and a chill ran through Angie because she knew he was angry and the whole meeting had gotten out of control. She was feeling a little anger herself. "I would've thought you would have had more understanding, if not for Angie then for your granddaughter—my daughter."

Doris puffed out her chest in indignation and ignored Hardy. "I guess you're going to let him see Erin and flaunt his paternity all over town," she said to Angie.

"Yes" was all Angie could say.

"Score one for mama bear," Patsy chanted and took a seat.

"AnaMarie, take me home." Doris stomped toward the door.

"Why are you so mad, Grandma?" Erin asked. "I've always wanted a daddy, and now I have one. A real daddy. And he wants me, too."

Hardy put an arm around Erin's shoulder as if to protect her.

"You're just a child and don't know what your mother has done."

"What did she do?" Erin lifted her shoulders in confusion. "She fell in love and made me. Don't you love me?"

Doris didn't respond. Then she suddenly turned and hugged her granddaughter. "Of course I love you. This is such a shock."

Erin took Hardy's hand and said, "Grandma, I'd like you to meet my daddy, Hardy Hollister."

Doris stared at Hardy. Angie held her breath.

"This will take some getting used to."

"That's okay," Erin said. "I'm not used to it either, but I love my mama and I know I'll love my daddy, too."

Doris choked back a sob and went out the door without a glance at Angie. AnaMarie was a step behind her.

AnaMarie glanced back. "She'll come around, Angie. Try not to worry."

Patsy sidled back over to Hardy. "So you were banging my eighteen-year-old sister? That really ticks me off."

"Give it a rest, Patsy, and I do not appreciate that language in front of Erin."

"Is banging what I think it means?" Erin asked.

Before Angie could find the proper words, Peggy got up and cupped Erin's face. "Patsy has no class. Pay no attention to her." She kissed the tip of Erin's nose. "You were conceived in love and we all love you."

"I love you, too," Erin replied in a low voice.

Peggy straightened and looked at her twin sister. "I'm going back to the apartment. You can find your own way home."

"You'd better not leave without me. I have no interest in Ray Goolsby. He has a big head. Have you ever noticed that? I should've charged him double for that haircut."

Peggy slammed the door in her face.

Patsy yanked it back open. "You'd better wait for me. I don't know why you like that bigheaded guy anyway. You…"

Angie closed the door, glad to shut out their conversation. Glad to shut out her family. She leaned against it, needing to regain her composure.

Erin reached for her crutches. "Time for ice cream."

Angie was always amazed at the resilience of children. How she wished she could bounce back so quickly. But there were a whole lot of years of her mother's criticism and judgment hanging over her head, and she'd never felt them more than today.

Hardy helped Erin into the kitchen. Their chattering went over Angie's head. She sank onto the sofa and wondered if she would hear her mother's words for the rest of her life. *You're such a disappointment. I will never forgive you for the disgrace you have brought to this family.*

Her angst probably came from years of trying to please her mother. She wanted to be the good girl her mother told everyone she was. But good only went so far until real emotions and human desires took over. She was not a prude, and she would not apologize for that night with Hardy no matter how much censure would be heaped on her in the next few days.

Hardy would feel the pressure, too. There was nothing like small-town gossip and small minds to derail his career. And she knew that was important to him and Judge Hollister. How would he handle the rumors and criticism?

What doesn't kill you makes you stronger. She'd heard that saying most of her life. By now she should have nerves of steel and superpowers to last her a lifetime. But the queasiness in her stomach belied that statement.

"Mama, can I call Jody?" Erin shouted from the kitchen. "I have to tell her."

"Okay. Fifteen minutes. That's it, and then it's time to get ready for bed. You've had a busy day."

"Aw, Mama, it's summer."

"And you're recovering from an accident."

"Mama always has an answer," Angie heard her whisper to Hardy and then giggle.

After a few minutes, Hardy came into the room and sat beside her. There was a love seat and several other chairs, and yet he chose the seat next to her. Six-foot-plus of all male was a little too close for her peace of mind.

"You okay?" he asked.

"I will be," she answered honestly. "It just takes a while to get used to this feeling in my stomach that I've disappointed my mother."

"I never realized your mother was so judgmental and narrow-minded."

"Mmm. My mother's mom was the same way, so I guess my mother had strict morals drilled into her from an early age. My older brother and sister left Horseshoe as soon as they graduated high school. My brother and his wife and four kids live in Houston, and my sister and her family live in Dallas. They rarely come home. Just on special occasions. I'll call them later and tell them what's happening in my life."

"I'm sure they'd appreciate that." He rubbed his hands together. "Grandma Ruby is certainly different. Your mom will probably never speak to her again."

"They've never gotten along. They've worked side by side in the bakery, yet they seem to hate each other and never miss a chance to show the other up. My mother's views on life are so stringent, and she expects her daughters to be the same way. Grandma Ruby is completely different. She was a lot of fun when I was growing up. She still is."

"Don't take this the wrong way, but I don't see Patsy or Peggy as good girls with strict moral values."

"They've always had that in-your-face attitude, and Mama had a hard time dealing with them. It's an ongoing struggle, as it is with Grandma Ruby, and it makes family gatherings difficult." She took a deep breath. "From now on, family gatherings will probably be pretty strange." She sat forward. "You know, I don't get it. Bubba has an apartment over the gas station and Margie Jansky stays there at least three or four times a week. My mother is aware of this. Yet she says nothing to Bubba. Why is that okay for a man?"

He shook his head. "I think it's expected of a man, but somehow the woman is supposed to be pure, especially in a small town."

"Well, screw that attitude."

"Angie, you're not exactly a femme fatale. We had a night together, and no one is going to think any less of you."

"I don't care what anybody thinks. I only care how this is going to affect Erin. Right now, she's all happy and bubbly. But earlier she was extremely hurt, and I just have this fear she's going to get hurt again."

His eyes caught hers. They were as dark as she'd ever

seen them. "I'm in her life now to see that that doesn't happen. You don't have to do this alone anymore."

She was stunned, and she had to admit a little grateful, that he was willing to take responsibility because there would be rumors and gossip. But he also had a life that did not include them.

"Thanks, but I can handle Erin and our lives. I'm not that naive young girl anymore." As hard as she tried, she couldn't keep the sarcasm out of her voice.

"I'm trying to make this right, Angie."

She pushed to her feet, needing to get away from him and his closeness. "Then spend time with your daughter and get to know her. That will make it right." She walked to the kitchen, leaving him staring after her. Her back felt hot from his scrutiny.

"Time's up," she told Erin.

"Gotta go," Erin said to Jody on the phone. "I'll see you in the morning."

Angie reached for a bottle of water out of the refrigerator. "Say good-night to Hardy."

Hardy stood with Erin's crutches in his hands. "Good night, peanut. I'll be back in the morning."

Erin took her crutches. "Okay," she replied, then looked up at Hardy with a strange expression Angie had never seen before. "Do you mind if I hug you?"

Hardy paled, but he recovered quickly. "No, of course not." He leaned over, and Erin put her little arms around his neck and squeezed. Hardy's hands shook as he held his daughter for the first time.

"You can't hug me too hard cause my ribs are still fractured," Erin told him.

Hardy leaned back and kissed the sterile strips on her forehead. "I'll never get over hitting you with my truck. My own daughter."

Erin smiled to take away his hurt, and Angie's throat clogged. "We'll remember it forever."

"Yeah. Sleep tight, peanut."

"Good night, Mr. Hardy, and thanks for the ice cream."

Hardy hesitated for a moment, and then walked out the back door. Angie wondered how long Erin would continue to call him Mr. Hardy. She probably didn't even realize she was doing it. It was just his name to her. It would be a while before she could say Daddy.

Angie and Erin made their way into the bedroom, and Angie helped her get ready for bed. Angie had to clean the incision on Erin's hip with antiseptic soap and put on a new bandage. In a pink-and-white gown, Erin hopped on one foot to the bed.

"Sweetie, I don't like you doing that. It's best to use the crutches. We don't want to do anything to impede the healing."

"Aw, Mama. I'm fine." Erin crawled into bed with all her stuffed animals around her.

Angie pulled the sheet up to Erin's chin and sat on the bed. Erin hadn't said anything about the explosive family meeting, and Angie didn't want her to harbor any bad feelings. "Grandma was a little upset tonight and didn't mean everything she said."

Erin brushed hair from her face. "Grandma doesn't take surprises very well."

"But she loves you." Angie was struggling to remember that, as well.

"I know, Mama."

"She's just mad at me."

"Mr. Hardy told her, didn't he? Grandma almost had a cow."

Hardy was a lawyer and used to debating and confronting people, but she was a little surprised that he'd taken on her mother. And touched. She shouldn't be, but sometimes emotions were hard to control. She knew that better than anyone.

Angie kissed her daughter. "Good night, baby."

"Mama, could you bring me paper and a pen? I want to write a letter."

"Now? You can do it tomorrow on my computer or my laptop."

Erin scooted up against the headboard. "I want to write it. It won't take long, and I'm not sleepy yet."

It was hard for Angie to refuse. She went to Erin's desk and got the paper, a pen and a book to write on. As she handed it to her, she saw the gum that Jody had brought her on her nightstand. She didn't like Erin chewing so much gum. It was bad for her teeth.

"I'll put this away." She scooped the gum into her hands.

"Okay," Erin replied without complaining. "It hurts my head to chew it now."

"You didn't tell me your head was hurting."

"Only when I chew gum, Mama. Chill."

Chill. She could do that. "I'm going to take a shower, and when I finish, it will be lights-out. You may not be tired, but I am. It's been a long day."

"Okay, Mama." Erin was already scribbling on the paper. Angie wondered what she was up to, but she didn't ask. Erin would tell her later.

Angie took a shower and brushed her hair out of its ponytail. Staring at herself in the mirror, she wondered how Hardy saw her today. The youthful Angie who had looked at the world through girlish fantasies was gone. She'd left her behind a long time ago with a broken heart and broken dreams. In her place stood a mature woman who was still struggling to find herself.

She'd taken a big step forward today by facing her mother. But repercussions would come. The town of Horseshoe would now judge her, but, unlike years ago, she'd have Hardy by her side. And they both would do everything they could to protect their child.

Over the past two years she'd seen Hardy with several women. Olivia had lasted longer than most. No one ever mentioned what had happened to his wife, and she never asked because it was none of her business.

She went to check on Erin, who was licking the seal of an envelope. "I finished, Mama."

"Where did you get the envelope?"

"Um…"

"Did you hop to the desk?"

"Yeah. It wasn't that far, and I was careful."

"Erin, what's so important about this letter?"

Erin looked down at the envelope in her hands. "It's a letter I wrote to the *Horseshoe Express.*"

"What? Why would you write a letter to the paper?"

Erin fidgeted for a minute. "Because I want to tell the people of Horseshoe about my daddy. I want them to know the real story."

"Erin." Angie sank down on the bed. "Let me read it."

Erin held the letter away. "No. I don't want you to read it until it's in the paper."

That threw Angie. Erin was never defiant or disobedient, and it was a little disconcerting to find her daughter taking a stand on something so serious.

"I can't let you put something in the paper unless I read it."

"You have to trust me, Mama. I deserve to have my say. Right?"

Angie stared at the stubborn eyes so much like Hardy's. "Erin—"

"It's not anything bad, Mama."

"Then why can't I read it?"

"Because…"

"What?" Angie asked.

"You might not let me send it."

Angie gazed at her daughter's beautiful face and knew she had to let Erin do this. For some reason it was important to her. She leaned over and kissed Erin's cheek. "Okay. I'll take it to the paper in the morning."

Erin shook her head. "Jody's coming on her bicycle in the morning, and she's taking it to the paper."

"Mmm. Does Peyton know this?"

Erin shrugged.

"Are you afraid I'll open the letter?"

"Maybe. Because you're always trying to protect me."

"Mothers do that." Angie stood. "Send your letter if it's that important to you."

"Thank you, Mama."

Angie turned off the light and walked out, wondering if she'd made the right decision. She paced in the kitchen. What was in the letter that Erin didn't want her to see? She turned out the kitchen light and went to her bedroom, but thoughts of the letter bothered her.

Unable to stop herself, she tiptoed to Erin's room. Her daughter was sound asleep. Moonlight streamed through the window. Angie saw the letter on the nightstand.

She reached out to take it. She could read the letter and Erin would never know. Angie would know, though. Her hand rested on the envelope for a moment. She couldn't do it. Her daughter had asked for her trust, and she had to give it even though it was difficult.

Silently, she trailed back to her room. Whatever was in the letter, she would find out along with everyone else.

But Hardy needed to know what was coming. She picked up her cell and called him before she changed her mind.

As she waited for him to answer, she realized this was the start of a new relationship for them—a relationship of parenting their child. She would now share that responsibility with him, and she wondered why it felt so right.

Chapter Ten

Hardy rested in a lounge chair at the pool, sipping a beer and watching the moonlight dance off the water in a dizzying display. He didn't come out here much. Every time he did, he thought of her: her smile, her laugh, her sunny disposition that lifted his heart in ways he couldn't describe. And in ways he didn't want to remember.

If he could go back, would he change what happened? Maybe not change, but he would certainly react differently. Neither of them was ready for marriage at that time and he wasn't sure what the future would've held for them if he'd known she was pregnant. He'd do the right thing; he knew that with all his heart.

He took a swallow from the bottle. Angie's mother was a fine piece of work. She hammered guilt into Angie like a nail into a coffin. Final. Complete. But Doris didn't count on Angie falling in love. His throat went dry at the thought. She'd loved him, and he'd let her down. Would he ever be able to overcome that?

Taking another swallow, he could almost hear her laughter as she'd run around the pool, trying to get away from him. They'd been happy in their own little world. How he wished it could have stayed that way.

His cell beeped and he picked it up from a side table. It was Olivia. He'd been trying to reach her.

"I'm sorry, Hardy," she said. "I've been in court all day. We're trying to wrap up this asbestos lawsuit. Was it anything important?"

"I need to talk to you."

"Sounds serious."

"It is." Hardy knew having a daughter was going to change his relationship with Olivia, but he was hoping she would adjust.

"Are you still agonizing over hitting that little girl?"

"Yeah, in a way. When do you think you can come to the ranch?"

"How about tomorrow? I need a break. I'll call Mavis and have her fix us a really nice dinner. I'll plan to spend the night."

"That sounds great." Olivia was a take-charge kind of woman, and he liked that about her. But as he watched the moonlight on the water, he wasn't seeing Olivia's face. It was Angie's. A young, vibrant Angie.

He closed his eyes, blocking out the image. They talked for a little bit and then he sat lost in his own misery. He'd worked for one goal all his life: to follow in his father's footsteps. It was all falling in place, but the feeling of elation wasn't there like it used to be. His mind was filled with regrets and doubts. He took another big gulp of beer.

His cell beeped again. He started to ignore it because he wasn't in the mood to talk to anyone. But he was a father now and he had to be responsible. Glancing at the caller ID, he saw it was Angie. He immediately answered.

"Anything wrong?" he asked.

"I don't know. I just needed to talk to you about something that's bothering me."

He sat up on the lounger because her voice sounded serious. "What is it?"

"Erin's written a letter for the paper and she won't let me see what's inside. She asked me to trust her. She says nothing bad is in it, but she wants the people of Horseshoe to know the truth about her father."

"I didn't expect this."

"Me, neither. I went into her room to get the letter and read it anyway. I planned to put it back without her knowing, but I couldn't do it. She wants me to trust her, and I'm finding that very hard to do. I just don't want her to get hurt or be embarrassed by people's reactions."

That the letter could hurt his political career ran through his mind briefly. His daughter wanted to voice her opinion, and he wasn't going to stop her, not even for his career. "Let's trust her."

"Are you sure? This affects you, too."

"After your mother's reaction, I'd say Erin's letter will probably be mild. Or at least I hope it is. Is she always this outspoken?"

"Yes, and I'm not sure where she gets that from. Certainly not from me."

"Dad is the most outspoken person I know."

"Oh, no, don't tell me she's going to be like Judge Hollister." She laughed. Hardy glanced at the water and saw a young Angie smiling at him. It was so real that for a moment he was caught in the past. *The beer must be more potent than I thought.*

"I'll come over first thing in the morning and talk to her. Maybe I can talk her into letting me read it. I don't want her to be embarrassed, either."

"I'll see you in the morning, then. And thanks."

"You don't have to thank me, Angie. We're in this together now."

There was total silence.

"It feels kind of surreal."

"Yeah. I'll see you in the morning." He held his phone for a little while and then slipped it into his pocket. This was what it was like to be a parent, sharing the responsibilities of a child with someone else. He hoped they could keep up the status quo, because above everything else he wanted Angie to be happy, as well as Erin. He would do everything he could to make that happen.

The next morning he was at Angie's before seven o'clock. Angie handed him a cup of coffee and he sat at the kitchen table. She wore a large Dallas Cowboys T-shirt and was barefoot. Her hair was tousled. He assumed she'd just gotten up. Maybe he shouldn't have come so early, but she didn't seem to mind. His eyes kept straying to her long legs.

He cleared his throat. "Anything new?"

"No, Erin is still asleep and the letter is still on her nightstand."

"Haven't been able to make yourself read it?"

She lifted an eyebrow. "Can you?"

He didn't get a chance to answer. AnaMarie rushed in with a plate of kolaches and placed them on the table. She hugged Angie. "Please call Mama. She's very upset and won't come to work at the bakery."

"I'm sorry, but she's the one who is so unrelenting."

"Angie—" Her eyes settled on Hardy. "Did you spend the night here?"

"He did not spend the night. Not that that's anyone's business."

"Sorry," AnaMarie apologized. "This is all so upsetting. Please just talk to Mama so life will be easier."

"I've given in to her so many times in the past, but this time I'm standing firm. Hardy is Erin's father, and soon everyone will know that and Mama will probably never speak to me again. So you'd better toughen up."

"Why is everyone in this family so stubborn? Now Grandma Ruby is at the bakery and I have to deal with her." AnaMarie went out the door grumbling and shaking her head.

"Mama," Erin called. "Who's here? I hear voices."

She lifted her eyebrow again. "You're up."

A knock sounded at the door before he could move. Angie opened it. Jody and her dog, Dolittle, stood there.

"Can I see Erin, please?" Jody asked.

Angie stepped aside. "She's in her room."

Jody ran for the hall, followed by the dog. Angie looked after them with indecision on her face.

"Thinking of eavesdropping?"

"Maybe, if I could figure out a way for them not to see me."

"Let's trust our daughter and stop agonizing over it. We faced your mother, so this should be a piece of cake."

Angie turned to refresh her coffee, but clearly her mind was on what was happening in Erin's room.

Jody came bouncing into the kitchen with a white envelope in her hand. "Gotta go. Bye."

"Does your mother know you're here?" Angie asked.

Jody shrugged. "She was changing J.W. and I told her I was going out."

"Out where?"

Jody shrugged again.

"Where's your dad?"

"He was shaving and getting ready for work. Gotta go. Bye." Jody made a quick exit with Dolittle on her heels.

"Interesting." Angie tapped her cheek with her forefinger.

Her cell buzzed on the counter, and she picked it up.

"She was just here." Obviously, it was Peyton. Angie told her what was going on.

"Erin roped Jody into doing this. Please don't be too upset with her."

Angie laid her phone on the counter. "Wyatt is on his way to find Jody," she told him.

"Jody is fine. She bicycles all over this town and everyone knows her."

"It's not that. She didn't tell them where she was going, and that's a big no-no."

Hardy's cell went off, and he fished it out of his pocket. Looking at the caller ID, he said, "It's Wyatt."

"I've got the letter and my wandering daughter." Wyatt came straight to the point. "Do you want me to bring the letter back?"

He glanced at Angie and saw a whole lot more than he wanted to in her eyes. She trusted him. His chest tightened. "No. We trust Erin, so let Jody take it in to the paper."

"Glad to hear you two are working things out."

"We're trying. Don't be too hard on Jody. This was our daughter's idea. She's struggling with the new revelations in her life, and we're glad she has Jody as a friend."

"Okay."

He clicked off. "We'll have to be on our toes to keep up with two conniving ten-year-olds."

"Yeah." Angie removed the plastic off the kolaches. "How about a sugar high?"

Out of the blue a different kind of high with her floated across his mind. He curbed those thoughts. "Why not?"

Erin hobbled into the room on her crutches. "Mr. Hardy, you're here."

He decided in that moment to be honest with his daughter. "Your mother called. Said you wrote a letter for the paper and asked how I felt about it."

Erin sank into a chair, and he took the crutches and

placed them against the wall. "I just want to tell people how I feel because this concerns me and Mama and no one else."

"How did you get so grown-up?"

"Mama raised me right." She rolled her eyes. "Grandma's always saying that, and I don't know what she means. All I know is my mama is a good person."

Angie kissed the top of her head. "And you're a good daughter. We should have matching T-shirts."

Erin giggled, then saw the kolaches. "Oh, boy, Ana-Marie's been here."

Angie poured milk for Erin, and they sat and had breakfast like a normal family. But they weren't normal, and in the next few days they would be tested with gossip and rumors. Through it all, and with a lot of prayer, maybe they could find normal in Horseshoe, Texas.

HARDY SPENT THE day at the house with Erin, doing everything she wanted, and Angie feared he was spoiling her. But sometimes maybe a kid needed spoiling. They were interrupted several times with phone calls from Olivia.

In the late afternoon, Hardy and Erin sat on the front porch, talking and playing on Hardy's phone. Hardy wanted to buy Erin one, but Angie was holding out. She wanted Erin to love Hardy for who he was, not for what he could give her. It was amazing how Hardy fit into their lives.

The paper came out once a week and was circulated on Tuesdays. Every bit of small-town gossip and community news was printed. She and Hardy were trying not to obsess about Tuesday.

It forced them, though, to face the problem of Judge Hollister. Hardy had to tell him. He'd been in Austin, and Hardy was waiting for him to return. They didn't want him to find out any other way but from them. It was going to be a shock to learn he had a granddaughter.

Angie went out to the front porch with a pitcher of lemonade. "Anyone thirsty?"

"Oh, boy, Mama makes good lemonade."

She poured a glass for everyone and sat on the stoop, drinking hers and relaxing on a windy June afternoon.

Hardy's cell buzzed and startled Erin, who was holding it. "You got a call." She handed the phone to him.

He stood and walked to the end of the porch to talk. In a second, he was back. "My dad is home. I think it's time for him to know he has a granddaughter."

Erin looked up. "You're going to tell him about me?"

"Yes. How do you feel about that?"

"I don't know. Judge Hollister makes me nervous."

Hardy squatted in front of her. "There's nothing to be nervous about. He's going to love you."

"You think so?"

"You bet." He glanced at Angie. "I have plans tonight, so I won't come back, but I'll see y'all tomorrow."

He hugged his daughter and strolled down the steps to his truck. Angie felt left out, and she knew she was being silly. But she could use a hug today—from Hardy. Where had that thought come from? That was a disaster waiting to happen.

As he drove away, she knew he was going to see Olivia. It was Saturday—date night. He hadn't told his girlfriend about Erin; he was probably doing that tonight, too. It was a big mess. The news was going to affect his relationship with the woman.

Just as she'd thought years ago, the news of his daughter would disrupt his life. The guilt weighed heavily on her, but there was no way to change things now.

HARDY SAW HIS dad's pickup in the garage and Olivia's Mercedes parked behind it. He took his time going into the house, rehearsing what he had to say. When he was growing up, his father had been bigger than life. Everyone respected him and looked up to him. So did Hardy. When his father pushed him to succeed, he did his best because he wanted to please him.

But constant schooling without a break wore him down. That was why he was so attracted to Angie. She brought calm to the storm in his life.

Like Angie had faced her mother, he now had to face his father. He was hoping that the news would be a turning point for them.

Mavis was running around like a crazed rabbit in the kitchen. She pulled rolls out of the oven. "The Duchess and the judge are in the library having drinks."

Mavis didn't like Olivia because Olivia gave orders and intended for them to be followed.

"Could you not call her the Duchess?"

She pierced him with a stare. "Could you tell her I'm not a gourmet cook and at her beck and call? Prime rib and all the trimmings for three people. Insane."

Hardy didn't know what else to say. Obviously Olivia had called with a menu. At other times he might see that as assertive and take-charge. Today wasn't one of those days.

His dad and Olivia were chatting as he walked in. Olivia came over and kissed him. He kissed her back, but there was something different about their chemistry, and he couldn't explain it.

"I thought you'd be home by now," Olivia said. "I had Mavis fix us a scrumptious meal and then we have the rest of the evening to ourselves."

"While I was in Austin at the club I talked to Judge

Swinson." His father handed him a glass of wine. "I also spoke to Judge Wycliff. He's a member, too. They both agree this is the time to throw your hat into the ring. Olivia and I were just talking about lining up some fundraisers and charity events you need to attend to get your name out there and to let people know you're running for judge in your district next November."

Hardy didn't have time to respond. Mavis entered the room. "Dinner is ready, and I would be pleased if you would eat so I can do the dishes and go home to my husband."

"There's no need to be testy," the judge told her.

"You haven't seen testy, Judge." She stormed back to the kitchen.

"I don't know why you keep that woman," Olivia said. "She's very rude."

"But reliable," the judge replied, making his way into the dining room.

Olivia had gone all out: china, crystal, silver and his grandmother's best linens. He sat at the right of his father. Olivia sat across from him. Mavis placed the food on the table and left without a word. The judge carved the prime rib, and they ate dinner. The conversation centered around Hardy's career.

As they talked, Hardy couldn't help but think of how warm and different it was eating in Angie's kitchen. Dinner with his father and Olivia suddenly seemed too stuffy and formal. The tension was about to get to him.

Hardy refilled their wineglasses and they slowly made their way into the living room. Before they could start discussing the election again, he said, "I have something to tell y'all."

Olivia sat on the sofa. "What is it?"

"I hope it's not something to do with Angie's daughter again." The judge took his seat in a wing-back chair. "You've spent entirely too much time away from the office, and it's time to get your mind back on business."

The censure stung. "I'm well aware of everything that goes on in the office. I'm on top of it."

"Every time I call you're not there."

Hardy took a sip of wine. "I have a cell, Dad, and you can reach me on it at all times." He swirled the wine around in the glass. "But that's not it, is it? You're checking up on me."

"I just don't want this accident to derail you. I know it was emotional hitting the child, but you have to get past it."

Hardy took a long breath. "It's hard to do that when you hit your own child."

The judge's eyebrows knotted together like one large caterpillar. "What the hell are you talking about?"

"Hardy, what are you saying?" Olivia asked.

He blew out a breath he didn't know he'd been holding. "I didn't know until the accident that Erin is my biological daughter."

"What the hell..." The judge was out of his chair in an instant.

"I have a daughter and she's ten years old. I've been spending time with her, getting to know her."

For the first time Hardy saw his father speechless. "Wh-what?"

"I have a—"

"I heard you the first damn time." His father's eyes narrowed. "You're not falling for that old trick? Angie said her kid is yours and you believe her?"

"I know she's mine."

"Did you have a DNA test done?"

"Dad, listen to me." Hardy sighed. "I don't need a DNA test. She's my kid."

"Are you drunk?"

Hardy wanted to laugh but refrained. His father was not in a laughing mood. "No. I'm telling you because the news is going to be all over Horseshoe on Tuesday. It's already leaking out, and I wanted you to hear the news from me."

"How the hell can you be the father of Angie Wiznowski's kid?"

"It doesn't matter. I am."

"Why didn't she tell you? Why are you finding out now?"

"I was in Europe when she found out and she was unable to contact me. That's all you need to know."

"Who's Angie?" Olivia carefully placed her wineglass on the coffee table.

"She's a friend of Rachel's," his father answered. "After my wife died, Angie and Rachel became very good friends."

Olivia looked at him. "And you and this Angie had an affair?"

Hardy wasn't discussing what happened between him and Angie. Maybe Olivia deserved the truth, but he was in no mood to share it now. "Erin is my daughter and that's all you need to know."

Olivia got to her feet. "Let me get this straight. You've known for a week that you have a child with this woman—a ten-year-old child, and you're just now telling me?"

"Yes. I've been trying to come to terms with it myself."

"If you had told me from the start, we could have done

something to combat the rumors that are sure to follow. Rumors that will hurt your run for office."

"I'm not thinking about the election. I'm thinking about a little girl who needs a father. My first priority was making sure she knew who I was. She does now, and we're making progress in our relationship. I want it to stay that way."

"You need to get your head straight and figure out what you want." Olivia reached for her purse on the sofa. "I've changed my mind about spending the night."

He walked her to her car in silence. The moonlight was bright with whispers of romance, but Hardy wasn't feeling too romantic. For some reason, he was feeling used.

She turned to face him. "This is going to hurt your election."

"Olivia, I have a kid. That means something to me."

She lovingly touched his chest. "I know, Hardy. I can hear it in your voice, but I'm not sure how this child is going to fit into your life—our lives. I'll be busy with the trial, so I won't call. I'll give you some time and maybe by the end of the week we can talk about the future. By then, maybe you'll see things differently." She reached up and kissed him. He didn't kiss her back. She got in her car and drove away, and he was left with a hollow feeling in his gut.

If this was love, it sucked. He went back into the house, knowing another confrontation was in store for him. His father didn't give up easily.

In the kitchen, Mavis was putting away pots and pans. She glanced at him. "The Duchess didn't take the news well, huh?"

Hardy leaned against the counter and folded his arms across his chest. "Were you eavesdropping?"

"Didn't have to. It's all over town that you're Erin's

father. Doris Wiznowski called, wanting to talk to the judge. I told her he was out of town and she asked for him to call her back. What do you want me to do with that information?"

Hardy shrugged. "Give the message to the judge." Doris could do all the bitching she wanted. It wasn't changing a thing.

Mavis folded a dish towel and laid it on the counter. "I remember that summer Angie was here. Nice, sweet, compassionate young woman. Rachel couldn't have had a better friend. You liked her, too. More than I realized."

"What are you getting at, Mavis?"

"Have you noticed the difference between Angie and Olivia?" She held up her two index fingers. "Two different worlds. You have to decide which world you want to live in."

"I haven't been asked to live in Angie's world."

"Yeah. There's that, but don't fool yourself. You'll be looking at those worlds very closely in the weeks ahead." Mavis removed her apron. "Now, I'm going home to Harvey, who's probably asleep in his chair." She patted his shoulder and walked out the door.

His life had been on course and he'd known exactly what he wanted. That all had changed. He wasn't even sure what his name was anymore. But he knew one thing for sure: he was not losing touch with his daughter. And Angie, well, that was just something he'd rather not think about. It made his head hurt with insecurities and doubts, which he rarely had.

"Hardy!" his father shouted.

Hardy pushed away from the counter and walked to his father's study.

The judge sat at his desk with his glasses perched on his nose, a pen in his hand and a pad in front of him.

"I've been talking to Will Strickler. He's a good family lawyer. We can do damage control. He'll make Angie a financial offer and we can get this swept under the rug."

Blood rushed to his face. "My daughter's name is Erin, and she will not be swept under the rug. Somehow I thought you would be thrilled to have a grandchild, but obviously I was delusional. Forget I said anything." He turned and left the room, wondering if that was all he was to his father—a means to an end to gain control of his seat on the bench. That was all that mattered to Hardison Hollister Sr.

But to Hardy, life was about a whole lot more—love and family. Everything had changed in a week. He was questioning everything he wanted. Everything he'd worked for. And everything that was the crux of his life. He had to decide if he could let go of a dream he'd had since he was a kid. Once he made that decision, there would be no turning back.

Chapter Eleven

Angie thought she would hear from Hardy after he talked to his father. She waited up until eleven and then went to bed. An ache in her stomach told her the news about Erin didn't sit well with Judge Hollister.

The next morning as she was making coffee, Hardy arrived. "Sorry it's so early, I wanted to see Erin."

"She's still sleeping." Unable to stop herself, she asked, "How did it go with your father?"

He heaved a sigh. "Not good. He wants a DNA test and I told him to stuff it."

Angie's stomach cramped. "How do you feel?"

His eyes caught hers. "What do you mean?"

"Do you want a DNA test?"

"No. I just have to look at her to know she's mine. There's never been any doubt about that."

She relaxed. "Thank you."

Staring into his deep blue eyes, she wanted to say so much more, but the words wouldn't come.

"Mama," Erin called. "Who's here?"

"Can I?" Hardy motioned toward the hall.

Angie nodded, and soon she heard Erin squeal. She was happy to see her father. Hardy didn't stay long, but he said he'd try to get back later. He had to meet with

Wyatt and several other leaders of the community to discuss Horseshoe's Fourth of July celebration.

As quickly as he had arrived, he was gone. Angie struggled with so many doubts and indecisions. But as long as she and Hardy stood firm together, they would be okay. The town gossipers and Judge Hollister didn't matter. *Oh, yeah, might need a dose of cough syrup to swallow that.*

The morning went smoothly. No one from the family stopped by; things were quiet. Peyton called and said that Wyatt had grounded Jody for two days. Now Angie had to entertain a bored daughter. At about eleven Erin went to sleep on her bed while they played Monopoly. Angie kissed her and went to fix lunch.

A knock at the door stopped her. She thought it was probably one of Erin's friends wanting to say hello. When she opened the door, she found Judge Hollister standing there with his cowboy hat in his hand.

Her heart jolted into her throat. "Good morning, Judge Hollister."

He inclined his head. "Morning, Angie. May I come in?"

Not even if hell was freezing over crossed her mind, but she stepped aside. "Have a seat," she said, being as polite as possible.

"No, thanks. This won't take long."

Angie tensed and prepared herself for whatever the man had to say.

"I hear you contend that your daughter is my son's."

"I don't contend. It's a fact."

"Are you willing to back that fact with a DNA test?"

"I don't have to. Hardy knows that Erin is his." Her eyes never left his face.

"Well, now, you see—" he looked down at the hat in his hand "—my son tends to be a little gullible at times."

"Then you don't know your son."

The old man never blinked. "I know my son better than you do. All his life he's had one goal and that is to follow in my footsteps. The election for my seat on the bench is coming up, and he has plans to run, but now with all this gossip he has very little chance of winning. You have derailed his dreams and you stand there like it means nothing."

Angie felt a crack in her demeanor. She knew of Hardy's aspirations for political office, but she thought it was more of what his dad wanted for him. Maybe it wasn't. Maybe she heard what she wanted to.

"I'm not apologizing for my daughter. Hardy had a right to know." Her words were strong, but her insides quivered like Jell-O.

"What happened to that right ten years ago?"

"I don't feel as if I owe you any explanation, and I'd appreciate it if you'd leave."

The judge looked at her long and hard. "Do the decent thing, Angie. Tell everyone you made up your daughter's paternity and let Hardy have his dream. Don't ruin his life."

The Jell-O turned to a bubbling rage at his audacity.

"Mama." Erin stood in the doorway on her crutches. A ball of fear replaced the rage. Had she heard those hateful words?

Trying to save face and trying not to hurt her daughter, she said, "This is Judge Hollister."

"I…know. I'm gonna get a glass of milk." She hobbled into the kitchen as if she sensed the tension in the room and wanted to get away from it.

The judge kept staring after Erin and made no move to speak. "Judge?"

"That's her?"

"Yes, that's Hardy's daughter." He seemed turned to stone. Angie just wanted him out of her house. She walked to the door and opened it. "Goodbye, Judge Hollister."

He glanced distractedly at her. "Huh?"

"Goodbye, Judge Hollister." She repeated.

This time he got the message and walked out, still with that stunned look on his face. Angie didn't have time to worry about him. She had to get to Erin.

Erin sat at the table, flipping through one of her books, drinking milk. "What did he want, Mama?" she asked when she saw Angie.

The urge to lie was strong, but she'd promised her daughter she wouldn't do that anymore. "He's a grouchy old man and not happy that I kept you a secret for so long."

"Why didn't he say hi to me?"

"I don't know, baby. Everyone needs time to adjust to the news."

"Mr. Hardy doesn't."

"No. He doesn't." She smiled through a sea of tears. She hadn't even realized she was on the verge of bawling like a baby.

"Everything's going to be okay," her child assured her as if she was the adult. It seemed her daughter was taking this better than she was.

"Now, what would you like for lunch?"

"Peanut butter and jelly on white bread. None of that healthy stuff."

Angie made a face but agreed on one condition. "We have to have fruit, too."

The rest of the day passed slowly, especially since Jody couldn't come over and Erin was confined to the house. Hardy called midafternoon to talk to Erin. Of course, she blurted out that Judge Hollister had been by. He immediately wanted to talk to Angie.

She was unsure of what to say, so she told him as little as possible. Telling him everything would only hurt him. And she was still struggling with what the judge had said and asked of her.

As she settled Erin down to watch a movie, she had to wonder if she was ruining his life. The revelation that Hardy had gotten a young girl pregnant and had no idea about the child could only hurt his reputation. And that was the last thing she wanted. The consequences of keeping her secret were now beating at her from all sides. She was the one who was hurting Hardy. It would hang over her for the rest of her life. But there was one thing she would not do: she would not lie again about Erin's paternity. The future looked so dim. She couldn't even see Hardy in their lives. Once the newness of this situation wore off, would he continue to come around or would his career take precedence?

ON MONDAY, HARDY had a full day at the office. He stopped to see Erin for a few minutes and called her at noon. He and Wyatt spent many hours interviewing witnesses on a convenience-store robbery getting ready to go to trial. It was after nine when he left the courthouse.

Streetlights illuminated the old two-story limestone courthouse. Age and weather had yellowed some of the stones. The courthouse was connected to the sheriff's office and jail. The buildings sat in the center of a town square that was in the shape of a horseshoe, hence the name for the town of about two thousand residents, give or take a birth or two. Gnarled live oaks and blooming red crepe myrtles enhanced the old structure that stood as a sentinel from generation to generation.

Backing out of his spot, he glimpsed the *Horseshoe Express* across the street in one of the old brick-and-mortar stores. He whipped into a space in front of it. He knew the paper was probably already printed and getting ready to distribute in the morning. To ease Angie's mind, he would try to finagle a copy.

The bell jingled over the door as he walked in. The smell of ink, dust and old paper greeted him. He could see Marlene and her husband, Wilbur, working in the back.

Marlene hurried to the counter. "Oh, Hardy, how can I help you?" There was a gleam in her eyes as if she knew something he didn't.

"I came to pick up a paper."

"They'll be out first thing in the morning."

His eyes didn't waver from hers. "I'd like to have one now." He reached for his wallet, pulled out a five and laid it on the counter.

She looked at the money and then at his face. Suddenly, a smile emerged. "Can't wait, can you?"

"No, ma'am. My daughter has written an article, and I'd like to be the first to read it."

She hurried to the back and returned with the paper rolled up and ready to distribute. Laying it on the counter, she said, "This is going to be the talk of the town for days to come."

He picked up the paper. "Not that long, I hope."

As he headed for the door, she called, "Congratulations."

Getting in his truck, he resisted the urge to open the paper. He wanted to read it with Angie. It was almost ten when he pulled into her driveway, yet the kitchen light was still on.

He tapped on the door, and she let him in. Yesterday she'd been hesitant to discuss his father's visit. The judge must have said something to upset her. He wanted to know what, but first they had to deal with the paper.

"Look what I have." He held up the paper.

Her eyes lit up. "You got a copy."

"Yes, ma'am." He looked around. "Where's Erin?"

"She's in bed. She wanted to wait until you came by, but she couldn't hold her eyes open any longer."

"Sorry. Wyatt and I got hung up at the courthouse."

"She understands." Angie glanced at the rolled-up paper in his hand. "Have you read it?"

"No. I wanted us to read it together."

"Oh." A look of surprise bracketed her face. "I'll make sure Erin is asleep, and then we'll read it." She hurried away. He followed to get a glimpse of his daughter.

He could barely see Erin for all the stuffed animals around her, but his child was sleeping peacefully with her long hair hiding most of her face. But that didn't matter. He knew she was there and safe.

Silently, they walked back to the kitchen.

He unrolled the paper. "Ready?"

"Yes." She sat at the table and he spread the pages out in front of her. A headline hit them immediately: The Secret of Horseshoe, Texas.

Neither said a word as they began to read.

My name is Erin. My mother is Angela Wiznowski. Everyone in Horseshoe knows us, but you don't know everything, and today I'm going to tell you all about me. You know that on my birthday I ran out into the street without thinking and was hit by Mr. Hardy Hollister. It was an accident and it was my fault. My mama has told me a hundred times to always check before I cross a street. I was having fun, though, and just wanted to get my ball.

That day changed my life. My mama has kept a secret for ten years, but after Mr. Hardy hit me she knew she had to tell the truth. You see, Mr. Hardy is my biological father. Yes, that's right. They fell in love years ago, but Mr. Hardy went to Europe and my mom went to school in Temple. When she found out she was pregnant, she couldn't reach Mr. Hardy and didn't know what to do. Things just sort of happened after that. My mom married someone else, but she didn't love him and it didn't work out.

At first, I was mad at her for not telling me. Then I realized she did what she always does. She protects me and takes care of me and loves me. She also taught me about Jesus Christ and forgiveness, so I wasn't mad for long. Everyone makes mistakes and she was really young. But she made a good life for us. I am a good kid. Everybody tells me that. I am a good kid because of my mama.

Some people will gossip and spread rumors. That's just their nature. There's a saying about living in glass houses. I don't know the rest of it but you know what I mean. My mama is the best. I am blessed to have her and now I will get to know my father, who already loves me. And when I get older and get in trouble or make a mistake, I know I can go to them and they will love and help me. I won't have to be afraid and alone like my mother was. I know that. That's all I have to say.

Erin

P.S. I told Mama about the letter and she wanted to read it. I didn't want her to, and I asked her to trust me. She did. Jody took it to Mrs. Marlene for me.

Total silence followed the reading. Angie got up and went to the cabinet for a dish towel and wiped her eyes.

"Why are you crying?"

"I don't know. She's so young and yet she seems so grown-up."

He nodded. "Our kid is something."

She wiped away more tears, and his chest grew tight at the sight. "There's nothing bad in the letter. She just wanted people in Horseshoe to know about her parents. She got it almost right."

Angie laid the towel on the counter. "Yeah, but at her age she shouldn't have to deal with the way I screwed up her life."

"Hey. We both screwed up, and now we get a chance to start over—for Erin."

"But our lives are different now."

There was something in her voice that bothered him. "What are you trying to say?"

"I'm saying we can't go back and be those people we were almost eleven years ago."

"No. We can't, but maybe we need to talk about that time."

She opened the refrigerator with a nervous movement

and then quickly closed it. "There's nothing left to talk about."

He knew there was, though. Neither had been willing to talk about it since Erin's accident. They both seemed intent on not discussing it. But now they had to. "Erin said that we were in love. I'm not sure that's correct. I know I cared for you deeply and looked forward to seeing you when I came home from school. Actually, it was the highlight of my life. But I was very aware you were infatuated with me and had a big crush on me. I did all I could to discourage that, even though I knew there was an attraction there. I accepted it for what it was because I needed you in my life at that time."

She leaned against the cabinet, not looking at him and not saying a word.

"I was so grateful for you helping Rachel to get over our mother's death. And I have to admit you helped me, too. I learned to laugh again and to feel joy. After our night together, I felt so much guilt because I took your innocence. You had your whole life ahead of you, and I couldn't get beyond the fact that I had taken something that didn't belong to me. Guilt is a powerful thing. I wanted to get as far away from you as possible because you reminded me of what had happened and what should not have happened."

She looked at him then, her eyes a molten gold, heated by the emotions inside her. "I gave you my innocence. You didn't take it. Let's get that straight. I know the difference. I was not infatuated with you. I loved you with all the fervor of an eighteen-year-old girl. It was very real to me, and every time I look at Erin I know it was love."

"Angie—"

"Make excuses for yourself, Hardy, but I know what happened that night was real."

He kept staring into the heat of her eyes, getting lost in the sweet essence that was Angie. He used to fight it, but tonight he had to admit she was right. What they'd shared had been real. Just as real as what he was feeling right now.

He stepped close to her and cupped her face with his hands. Her skin was as smooth as anything he'd ever touched. He was always afraid to touch her, almost as if it was forbidden. He never understood why until that moment. Because she was the only woman who could make him lose himself. And he prided himself on control. Losing it for a second had brought on the guilt.

"It was real for me, too," he whispered against her lips.

"Then why deny it?" Her breath fanned his skin, and he could feel himself being pulled back into the magic that had brought him out of the dark days of his mother's death.

"I always felt I had to because I was older."

She wrapped her arms around his waist, and his lips took hers in a well-remembered passion. She tasted of cinnamon and chocolate, and he knew she'd been eating something from the bakery. The sweetness changed almost immediately as the kiss deepened.

She moaned deep in her throat, and he was lost with wanting more and more. He had been denying himself for years. Just when he thought they were on the same level, she pulled away and rested her forehead on his chest for a minute. Then she stepped away.

A coolness invaded his system and the molten gold of her eyes was now tepid.

"Angie..."

She tucked a strand of hair behind her ear. "What are we doing, Hardy? You're involved with Olivia. We can't go back. We have to go forward."

He had no idea where her head was, and he wasn't thinking straight, either. All he knew was he wanted to be with her and he wanted to make the past right once again because he wasn't going away.

"We can make the future better."

"Please..."

He threw up his hands and stepped back, knowing it was time to call it a night. He was tired and so was she. He didn't want to say anything to hurt her or change their relationship. He had to share an amicable peace with her for Erin.

"Okay. I apologize for kissing you. I was out of line, but we still have a lot to resolve about the past. But it can wait." He tapped the paper on the table. "Tomorrow we'll have to deal with this."

"Thank you for bringing it over." Her words were stilted, as if they'd never shared a passionate kiss. And then he realized she was fighting the attraction. She was right, too. He had no business kissing her.

He turned toward the door. "I'll see you tomorrow."

She didn't say anything, and he walked out. In the warm night air, he stood for a moment and wondered what was wrong with him. He was planning a future with one woman and kissing another. He had reached a new low.

Chapter Twelve

Angie stood in the middle of the kitchen with her fingertips touching her lips, remembering the sensual feel of Hardy's against hers and being enclosed in a powerful aura that was him. She thought she'd forgotten the gentle touch of his hands, the passion of his lips and the power of his body against hers. But it was right there at the edge of her consciousness, waiting to remind her that some things were unforgettable.

After picking up the paper, she went to her room, showered and crawled into bed. Thoughts of Hardy plagued her. Why was it so hard for him to admit that he might have loved her back then? Maybe he thought she wanted a commitment from him now. But she had made it abundantly clear that she didn't. And then there was Olivia. She flipped over in bed. The man was driving her crazy in more ways than one.

She wasn't sure when she went to sleep. The buzz of her cell woke her. She fumbled around for it on the nightstand and saw it was 5:00 a.m. Who could be calling this early? She clicked it on.

"Angie, have you seen the paper?" It was Peyton.

"It's five in the morning."

"I know. I was up with J.W. and saw the lights of the car when they threw the paper. Of course, I had to go out and get it in my sexy nightie. Wyatt said he was going to arrest me for indecent exposure."

Angie scooted up in bed. "Peyton, it's five in the morning."

"You've already mentioned that. I thought you wanted to read the article."

"Hardy brought it by last night and we read it together."

"Ah, crap, I woke you for nothing."

"But I appreciate the gesture."

"It was a lovely article, and you had nothing to worry about. Think I'll wake Jody and tell her she's not grounded anymore."

"She'd probably be happier if you waited until about eight."

Peyton chuckled. "I'm just happy for you. I'll call you later."

Angie trudged out of bed, brushed her teeth and went to the kitchen. She knew she wouldn't be able to get back to sleep. The people of Horseshoe would have a little excitement with their breakfasts, and she needed lots of coffee to brace herself for what was to come.

WHEN HARDY REACHED the ranch, everything was in darkness except for the outside lights. He bounded upstairs, took a shower, slipped into a bathrobe and hurried downstairs to the kitchen. After grabbing two beers, he went outside to the pool. The night air embraced him as he stretched out on a lounge chair, sipping a beer and watching the moonlight on the water. It was relaxing.

So many feelings churned inside him. Angie seemed to know what she'd felt all those years ago, even though she had been very young. He, on the other hand, had a hard time rationalizing anything he'd felt at the time.

All he knew was that he had liked her and wanted to be with her.

Erin had written that her parents were in love. The thought seemed to dance with the moonlight across the water. And then it hit him. He was afraid to admit he'd loved her because that would have required something from him more than a disappearance.

He downed the rest of the beer, not liking what he was thinking. How could Angie know what he was feeling without him even being aware of it?

Back then if he'd admitted the truth to himself, life would have been so different. But he couldn't go back. Nor did he want to. He and Angie had to talk. She'd become so angry when he'd mentioned infatuation. He had to let her know that's the way he had to view their relationship for him to deal with his own emotions. It was all about him and what he'd done to her. Guilt was hammering him once again.

He awoke at four and realized he was still in the lounge chair by the pool. His stiff muscles reminded him he was getting too old to sleep in lounge chairs. He went upstairs and got dressed for court. But before work, he had something to do.

He drove to the cattle guard and got the paper, which had been delivered earlier in the morning. When he returned, his dad was sitting at the kitchen table, nursing a cup of coffee. Hardy unrolled the paper and laid it in front of him.

"Thought you might like to read what your granddaughter had to say."

His father fished his glasses from his shirt pocket and began to read. When he didn't say anything, Hardy asked, "Well?"

The judge looked at him. "What do you want me to say?"

Hardy threw up his hands. "Nothing, Dad." He headed for the door, but he couldn't let it go. He swung back. "What did you say to Angie?"

"Didn't she tell you?"

"No, but I could tell she was upset."

The judge removed his glasses. "Yeah. I should have never gone over there."

"Why did you?"

His father slipped the glasses back into his pocket. "I was trying to save your future."

"What?"

"I asked her to say she lied about the girl's paternity."

Anger slammed into his chest. "You did what?"

"You've worked your whole life toward one goal, and I thought you were throwing it away. I had to do something. But then I saw the girl."

Some of the anger left him at the anguish in his father's voice. "And?"

"She's your daughter."

"I told you that. Why is it so hard for you to believe?"

"Because you're throwing away your whole damn future!" the judge yelled in the voice known to make strong men weak. "At least, that's the way I saw it on Sunday. Now I can't get that little girl's face out of my head. She has the Hollister blue eyes."

All the anger faded as he stared at his strong father admitting he was wrong. That had to be a first.

"Yes, she has the Hollister eyes, and she is the sweetest little thing you would ever want to meet."

The judge looked up. "When can I meet her?"

"I'll ask Angie."

"You know, it's not all up to Angie. You have some say here, too."

He took a couple of steps toward his dad. "It's all up to Angie, and it's all about Erin's best interests. I will do nothing that will cause either of them any more pain or hurt. And I want you to stay away until you're in a better frame of mind. If you want to be part of my child's life, you have to follow the rules. My rules. And I want you to apologize to Angie." He walked out, feeling for once that maybe he had gotten through to his father.

By seven, he was at Angie's. He wanted to spend some time with his daughter before he went to the courthouse. Angie handed him a cup of coffee—he was getting used to having coffee with her in the mornings.

It was going to be a hot day, and Angie was dressed in shorts and a sleeveless knit top. His eyes kept straying to her slender arms and long smooth legs. Her hair was up in its usual ponytail, which bounced around when she moved. She had an energy about her that was spellbinding.

"I'm sorry if I hurt your feelings last night." He wanted her to know that before the day crowded in on her.

She leaned against the cabinet, her breasts pressing against the taut knit top. "I'm not eighteen anymore, and it takes a lot to hurt my feelings, so you don't have to worry about that. I can take it."

"Tough, huh?" He grinned over the rim of his cup.

"Maybe." She cradled her cup in her hands. "May I ask you a question?"

By the tone of her voice, he knew it was personal. *No* circled his mind, but what he said was, "Sure."

"What happened to your marriage?"

That he wasn't expecting. It was personal. Private. None of her business, really, but he wanted them to be honest with each other. "I met her in Paris. She was a buyer for Neiman Marcus. We hit it off from the start, and neither of us saw the problems ahead. She traveled a great deal. I was involved in building my law career, so we rarely saw each other. It didn't take long for us to realize it was over." He took a deep breath and forced himself to tell the rest. "And I had a lot of unresolved issues about you."

She lifted an eyebrow. "Me? We didn't have any issues. We had sex. Period. You had a ton of guilt, though."

"Okay. You were right about infatuation. I needed your feelings to be an infatuation."

"Mmm." She took a sip, watching him. "That way it made what we did wrong. That way you took advantage of me and my feelings. That way you could feel all the guilt that you wanted. But once you admitted that I loved you, it would change things. It would make it right and natural. But what would you do with all that guilt? You needed to feel the guilt for some reason known only to you."

"Yeah," he admitted.

"Now you have to admit how you really felt back then."

He stared into her honey-brown eyes that seemed to know everything. "I thought about it last night and I know how I really felt. I'm not afraid to admit it anymore."

She set her cup on the counter and turned slightly, as if she didn't want to hear what he had to say. "I…"

"Mama, I hear voices. Is Mr. Hardy here?"

Angie headed toward the hall. "I'll help her get dressed."

And just like that, she had escaped what he was about to admit. He poured another cup and sat down, feeling hurt and not understanding why. Or maybe he did. So much had happened in the past few days, he was struggling just to keep his head on straight.

"Mr. Hardy, I thought that was you." Erin hobbled into the kitchen, and Hardy got to his feet, wondering if she was ever going to call him anything other than Mr. Hardy.

Erin looked around the kitchen. "Isn't the paper here?"

"I'll get it," Angie said and ran for the front door. Erin wanted to watch them read it, so they'd pretend for her.

The three of them sat at the table and read the article.

"What do you think?" Erin asked, beaming with excitement.

Angie kissed her cheek. "You did a great job. Now you have to prepare yourself for everyone's reaction."

"Don't worry, Mama. I can handle it."

"I'm proud of you, peanut," Hardy told her.

"I wonder if Grandma will read it?" Erin fidgeted in her chair, obviously upset by her grandmother's absence over the past few days.

Angie wrapped her arms around Erin from behind. "Like we said, it's going to take a little adjusting for everyone."

The door opened, and Patsy and Peggy burst in dressed in colorful shorts and tank tops. Their bleached and colored hair stuck out like straw, reminding Hardy of scarecrows.

"Have you seen this?" Patsy slapped the paper on the table.

"Of course, Aunt Patsy. I wrote it," Erin answered before he or Angie could find their voices.

Patsy pulled Angie aside, but Hardy could still hear them, as could Erin. "Why did you let her do this?"

"Not that I owe you an explanation, but she wanted to. This situation hasn't been easy for her, and she wanted to express her feelings. I allowed it. Now I'm wondering why you're running around Horseshoe in your night clothes."

Patsy blushed, to Hardy's amazement. "We had a little party for Bighead and his friend last night."

"And Mama's worried about *me* disgracing the family," Angie scoffed.

"You're her favorite. She expects better from you."

"Oh, please."

Peggy plopped into a chair. "I have a tremendous headache. And, Patsy, you're making it worse. I told you Angie knew."

"Mama hasn't been out of the house and when she reads this, we'll never get her out of there." Patsy placed her hands on her hips. "And it's all your fault." She glared at Hardy.

Something in him snapped at her rude behavior. "I'd appreciate it if you take your attitude somewhere else. You're upsetting Erin, and that gets me upset. So if you want to take this outside, you can yell at me all you want. Let's go."

"Stop it!" Angie yelled. "Patsy and Peggy, go home. I'll take care of Erin, and y'all can mind your own business. And, please, don't come back until you learn some manners."

Patsy touched her forehead and frowned. "I'm half-asleep and I don't know what I'm doing."

"I'll buy that," Angie said, taking her sister's arm and pushing her toward the door.

Patsy ran back and hugged Erin. "I'm sorry, Cupcake."

Erin didn't respond. Hardy's temper rose at what this was doing to his daughter.

Angie quickly got her sisters out of the house and sat

down by Erin. "Sweetie, she didn't mean anything. She just worries about you."

Erin reached for her crutches and went into the living room. Angie looked at him, and he shrugged. Then they both followed her. Erin sat on the sofa, tears rolling down her cheeks.

Hardy's heart constricted at the sight. Angie sat on one side of her and he on the other. Angie wrapped her arms around their daughter.

"Hey, hey, what are all the tears about?"

"Everybody hates me."

Angie kissed Erin's forehead. "No, they don't, baby. They love you."

"Grandma doesn't. She won't even come over here anymore. And Grandpa Hollister won't even speak to me. What did I do wrong?"

Hardy could barely stand it. He wrapped his arms around her, too, trying to give her some comfort. "Listen to me. You've done nothing wrong, and I don't want you to feel that way. Your mother loves you. I love you. So please put a smile on your face or I'm going to start crying, too."

Erin hiccuped and a giggle bubbled through. Suddenly, she wrapped her little arms around his waist. "I love you, too, Daddy."

His heart stopped completely. He looked into Angie's tear-filled eyes and the world tilted. Maybe for the first time in the right direction. He kissed the top of Erin's head. "No matter what happens today, we're in this together. I'm always going to be here for you now. Remember that, and don't let anyone steal your joy at finding your father. Because then I'll have to beat them to a pulp."

Erin giggled and wiped away tears.

"You okay?" he asked.

His cell buzzed and he cursed to himself, but he pulled it out and saw it was his secretary. "Work is calling."

"It's okay," Erin said.

He ignored it. His daughter needed him. His cell buzzed again. Wyatt this time. *Damn it!* He had a trial about to start and had to face his responsibilities to the county. He was the D.A.

"I'll be back as soon as I can, and I'll call when I get a break."

Erin leaned into her mother, and Angie stroked her hair.

He hated to leave, but he had no choice. He reached down and kissed her again. "Call me if you get upset, and I'll call you back as soon as I get free. I'll even leave the courtroom if I have to."

His daughter nodded. He forced himself to walk to his truck and go to his job—the last place he wanted to be.

ANGIE WRAPPED HER arms around her daughter and just held her. "What would you like for breakfast? How about French toast?"

"I'm not hungry," Erin mumbled into Angie's chest. "Aunt AnaMarie always brings me something from the bakery. She didn't come this morning."

"You know I've been letting you eat a lot of sweets lately because you needed a pick-me-up, but it's time to get back to eating healthy. Besides, it's busy at the bakery in the mornings."

"That's why AnaMarie comes early."

"I'm going to fix us the best breakfast ever." Angie kissed her child and got to her feet, her heart as heavy as it had ever been. In the kitchen she grabbed her phone and called AnaMarie, intending to give her an earful, but her sister breezed in.

Angie laid down her phone. "You just saved your own life. I was thinking of ways to throttle you."

AnaMarie looked confused. "Why?"

"One little niece is missing her aunt's attention."

"Things are crazy this morning. Grandma Ruby is making me nuts." AnaMarie looked around. "Where's our baby?"

Angie pointed to the living room.

AnaMarie hurried away with a plateful of cupcakes.

Erin squealed, and the world grew brighter. Angie opened the refrigerator and poured her daughter a glass of milk. This day had to get better. As she sat with Erin, eating chocolate cupcakes with chocolate-cream-cheese icing, which cured just about everything, she thought about Hardy and his job. It took precedence over them— over Erin. It was insane for her to think such a thing. She knew he had a stressful job and he couldn't just not show up, especially with a trial coming up.

Judge Hollister's words came back to her. *Don't ruin his life.*

THE REST OF the day went smoothly. Patsy and Peggy came back and apologized profusely until Erin had them eating out of her hand. They would've turned cartwheels if she had asked.

Bubba showed up and then her father, but her mother was absent. She was sure Erin noticed it, too.

Mrs. Wimby was the first to knock on the door. She brought Erin's ball back. Angie had completely forgotten about it. Then Mrs. Satterwhite, Mrs. Hornsby, Mrs. Peabody and every neighbor within a two-block radius came to say how proud they were of Erin and her courage. It gave her daughter a chance to talk about her fa-

ther. And that made Erin happy. It was a long day with
Angie continually going to the door.

Late in the day she answered it one more time and was
surprised to see Judge Hollister standing there with his
hat in his hand again.

"I know I said some things I shouldn't have, but I'm
known for that. Big mouth and all. I am sincerely sorry I
asked you to do such a terrible thing. I hope you can forgive me and allow me to see my granddaughter."

Staying upset with Judge Hollister would accomplish
nothing, and Erin needed to know her grandfather cared
about her.

"Mama, who is it?" Erin called.

She opened the door wider. "It's your grandfather."

"Oh." Erin's eyes rounded in disbelief.

Judge Hollister stared at her. "It's nice to meet you,
Erin." He walked into the room.

"It's nice to meet you, too." Erin said what was expected of her, but she fidgeted. A sign she was nervous.

Judge Hollister glanced at Angie. "Do you mind if I
sit down?"

Angie shook her head, and he eased into a chair by
Erin. "You have the Hollister eyes."

"I do?"

"Yes, you do. They're just like your father's and mine."

Angie tiptoed into the kitchen and let Erin have this
time with her grandfather. She was positive Judge Hollister would not say one word to hurt her. Evidently Hardy
had talked to him, and that warmed her heart.

"Mama," Erin called. Angie went back into the living
room. "Grandpa Hollister says they have horses at his
ranch and, when I get better, I can come and ride one."

"That would be nice." Angie would not keep her child
from her father or his family. Not ever again. Erin's eyes

sparkled, and that was all that mattered. But she had a foreboding sense her child was slipping away from her, which was ridiculous. No one could take Erin from her.

Judge Hollister soon left with a promise that he would be back. Erin chatted nonstop about how nice he was, not scary at all. Angie wanted to laugh at that, but she didn't because she knew Judge Hollister could be scary as hell when he wanted to be.

A day that had started out dramatically had ended perfectly. Erin was bubbly and chatty, talking to Hardy on the phone and telling him about her day. She went to sleep with a smile on her face.

That set the pattern for the next few days. The letter in the paper did more than anything Angie could have done. The people of Horseshoe saw their actions through the eyes of a little girl, and it changed everything. The days that followed were busy with Erin's friends coming and going. Jody was back, and Erin was her usual cheerful self.

Hardy went with them for the checkup to the doctor. Everything was right on schedule. They took X-rays of Erin's chest and leg. The doctor said Angie didn't have to tape Erin's chest anymore. He also removed the surgical tape on her forehead and said the stitches on her hip were dissolving nicely. It was good news, and Hardy wanted to take them out to dinner to celebrate. Angie declined. They weren't a family. She didn't want to give Erin false hope that they could be. That's what she told herself, but she had a hard time convincing her heart.

They ended up stopping for hamburgers at a McDonald's, and that was all it took to make Erin's day. It wasn't a place she or Hardy would've chosen, but neither complained. It probably was the first time she'd ever been out with Hardy outside the ranch and it felt a little sur-

real and perfect at the same time. At the back of Angie's
mind, though, she wondered how Olivia would feel about
him taking her out to eat.

Hardy said very little about Olivia, and Angie didn't
press him. It was his business. If and when it affected
Erin, she would speak up. For now things were amicable.

Hardy left Angie's and headed into Austin. He'd given
Olivia a few days to calm down and he needed to talk
to her. He had to be back in court in the morning, so he
couldn't stay long.

When he reached her apartment, he could hear voices
inside. He rang the doorbell. Olivia answered. Her eyes
lit up when she saw him. She went into his arms and
they kissed.

"I'm sorry I was testy the other day," she said. "I think
I was in shock."

He was relieved at her words. He was still feeling
a little shock himself. Laughter came from within her
apartment. "Do you have company?"

"We got a verdict on the asbestos case." She reached
up and kissed him again. "A big settlement and we're
celebrating. Come in, I'll introduce you."

He followed her into the living area. Five other people were in the room, three men and two women. Olivia
made the introductions, and he shook hands all around.
A glass of wine was shoved into his hand as talk turned
to their victory. Hardy felt a little out of place.

"Can I talk to you?" he whispered in her ear.

She took his hand and led them into her bedroom.
She stepped into his arms, and they shared a long kiss.
"I've missed you."

"Me, too." In a way he had, so he wasn't lying.

She looked up at him. "We're going out to a club to

celebrate. Come with us. We'll have a great time and put all the heartache aside for a while."

That hit him the wrong way. "My daughter is not a heartache."

"Hardy, I didn't mean it that way." She stepped away from him. "This is going to take time to get used to."

"Every day I see my daughter it just gets better and better. I don't know how else to say it. I thought fatherhood would scare me to death, but it's becoming very natural."

Olivia brushed back her blond hair with a nervous hand. "Are you seeing the mother, too?"

"Of course. Erin lives with her."

Olivia sat on the bed. "Do you still have feelings for her?"

The question caught him off guard and *no* ran through his mind only to be mocked by his common sense. "I like Angie. I've always liked her. She's a warm, loving, compassionate person and—"

"Oh, God, I'm going to gag."

"We share a child."

"A little fact she forgot to mention for ten damn years." She stood quickly. "This is changing you, and it's changing your life. Your campaign. Everything. I would think you would be extremely angry."

He took a deep breath. "I was for a while, but all I have to do is look at Erin and the anger goes away."

"I don't know what you want me to say, Hardy. I'm having a hard time with this."

"I can see that. Maybe we need to take a break until I get my life sorted out."

She stepped closer to him and placed her hands on his chest. "Let's go out tonight and enjoy the evening. Just the two of us and forget about all the problems."

"You mean forget about my daughter."

Her eyes flashed with anger. "You always come back to that as if you want to shut me out."

"Olivia, this has been a very difficult time and—"

"Forget it, Hardy. I'm going out tonight and enjoying myself with or without you." She stomped out of the room. He stood there for a moment, wondering if his life was ever going to get back on track.

He left without speaking to her again, and he knew that their relationship was over. She might not admit it and it might take a while to sink in, but he knew Olivia was not going to accept his daughter. Without that, they had no relationship. It was that simple.

THE NEXT WEEK Hardy was in court every day, and Angie and Erin saw very little of him. He stopped by in the mornings and late at night to talk to Erin. Angie was also back at work and busy. It was what she needed to get her mind on something else.

That evening Hardy was in a good mood because he'd gotten a conviction on the robbery case. His dark blue eyes gleamed when he talked about his work. He really enjoyed putting criminals behind bars, and Angie couldn't help but think he'd make a good judge.

Erin was in her room, talking to Jody on the phone, and they were sitting on the sofa. He had on his customary jeans, white shirt and boots. During a trial he wore a suit, but most of the time he was in pressed jeans and white shirts. The shirts were always long-sleeved, and he filled them out better than any man she'd ever seen. The cotton fabric stretched tight across his broad shoulders, and she thought she could look at him all day long.

"Erin will be off the crutches soon. I'd like to take

her out to the ranch," Hardy said. "Actually, I have orders to bring her."

She collected her wandering thoughts and settled back in the corner of the sofa. "What made your father change his mind?"

"When he saw her eyes, he knew Erin was mine, and that changed his whole attitude. I'm not saying the controlling, manipulative man is gone, but he's easier to deal with." He glanced at her. "I'd like for you to come with us."

For a moment she was completely mesmerized by the warmth of his eyes and the temptation to agree was strong. But her time at the ranch was over. She couldn't go back. She wouldn't go back. "I think this is father-daughter time, and I have tons of work to catch up on now that Erin is so much better."

Strong lines of concern were etched in his face. "It would be easier for Erin if you came."

Her heart raced and she hated herself for being so gullible. "It might be a good time to introduce her to Olivia." Did she just say that? Oh, the things she did for her daughter.

He rubbed his hands together. "Olivia and I are taking a break."

"Because of Erin?"

He looked at her levelly. "She has to accept my kid or we have nothing."

"I'm sorry, Hardy." Everything she feared was coming true. She was ruining his life. His plans. His dreams. She never wanted that to happen. Damn fate. Damn everything that made her feel so guilty. So vulnerable. So helpless.

The phone rang and Angie jumped up to answer it. Hardly anyone called her on the landline, and she'd been meaning to take it out. It was probably a telemarketer. She was in a hurry to get off the phone to assure Hardy...of what? She wasn't sure. She just wanted to get rid of the guilt that rode her conscience.

"Is this Angela Wiznowski?"

"Yes."

"This is Sharon Dunlap. I'm with Child Protective Services."

Angie froze for a moment. "What is this about? Do you have the right person?"

"Do you live in Horseshoe, Texas, and have a ten-year-old daughter named Erin?"

A shiver of alarm shot through her. "Yes."

"I'd like to talk with you at your earliest convenience."

"What is this about?"

"I'd rather not talk about it on the phone. Do you have any time tomorrow?"

"How about two o'clock in the afternoon?"

"That will be fine. I have your street address. I'll call if I get lost."

"Where are you coming from?"

"Austin. I'll see you tomorrow and explain everything."

Angie hung up with an uneasy feeling.

"What is it?" Hardy asked.

"It was a lady from Child Protective Services and she wants to talk to me."

"Did she give you a reason why?"

"No, and I have a really bad feeling about this. Child Protective Services protects children from abuse and neglect. Why would they want to talk to me? Unless..."

"What?"

Her eyes narrowed. "Unless someone called them to file a complaint about how I raise Erin."

"Who..." He quickly got to his feet. "You think my father might have called them?"

"Would he do that? Would he try to take Erin from me?"

"Angie." He pulled her into his arms, and she felt safe, as if nothing could come between her and her child. "I would never let him do that. Please believe me. I'll talk to him, but let's wait and see what the lady has to say."

"Okay." She raised her head and he bent toward her. Her lips were starved for the touch of his, and she really needed him tonight. Even though it was wrong. Even though he was with someone else.

"It's time for ice cream," Erin shouted from her room.

Hardy groaned and rested his forehead against hers. Laughing, they walked to the kitchen. But the uneasiness wouldn't go away. Angie still had that bad feeling in her stomach, as if her world was about to be shattered once again.

Chapter Thirteen

By the time Hardy reached the ranch, his dad was in bed. He planned to question him in the morning, but he believed his dad wouldn't do something so devious. His father was already forming a connection to Erin. Unless he'd deemed, in his own mind, that Hardy should have full custody. *Damn!*

Hardy didn't sleep much. He was up early, waiting for his dad to make an appearance. It didn't take long. The judge was an early riser.

Leaning against the counter, Hardy sipped his coffee. He waited until his dad got a cup and sat at the table. Mavis was somewhere else in the house, and it was the perfect opportunity.

"Have you made arrangements for Erin to come visit us?" his dad asked.

"Not yet." Hardy pulled out a chair and sat facing his father. "I'm going to ask you a question, and I want you to answer honestly."

The judge's eyebrows knit together. "Why would I answer any other way?"

"Did you call Child Protective Services about Erin?"

"Why would I do that?"

"I don't know. Maybe for the same reason you asked

Angie to deny I was the father. Don't act all indignant. I just want an answer."

"No."

Hardy stared into stubborn blue eyes just like his, and knew he wasn't lying. A feeling of relief surged through him. He was tired of fighting his dad. He was tired of so many things.

"Good. I want us to have a good relationship with Angie for Erin's sake."

Instead of answering, the judge took a sip of coffee, his eyes never leaving Hardy's. "Are you sure it's not more than that?"

"What do you mean?"

"You're spending a lot of time at Angie's and you've forgotten about your campaign. You have to get back to business. We'll hire publicists to make the announcement about Erin, and it should get the attention of the voters and pull on a few heartstrings. At first, I thought it would hurt your campaign, but I'm revising that decision. People love human-interest stories and it will certainly get your name in front of the voters."

Hardy groaned and got to his feet. "I'll see you later." He couldn't be angry at his father for championing his career because Hardy had made it clear since he was a boy that was what he wanted—to follow in his dad's footsteps. But now so many things were pulling at him and he wasn't sure exactly what he wanted. A grown man should know what he wanted without any doubts. Without any guilt. Without any heartache. Was that possible for him?

He was at Angie's early because he wanted to reassure her she didn't have anything to fear from the Hollisters. She wore a yellow-and-white sundress that came just above her knees. Her hair was loose around her shoulders—she rarely wore it that way. He stared at the glow in her eyes and thought how beautiful she was. He'd never really thought of her as beautiful, but at that moment he saw the woman she'd become: strong, mature and incredibly attractive.

He loved being with her in her kitchen, watching her, soaking up the calmness that was a part of her. Well, usually. Today she was nervous and edgy, going from the refrigerator to the stove and back to the table.

He caught her arms and stopped her. "Please calm down. I have to go to work, but I plan to be back in time to talk to the lady with you. I won't let you do that alone."

"Thanks." The sadness in her eyes tore at him.

"No one is taking Erin. You have my word on that. I'm a lawyer and the D.A., remember?"

She smiled slightly, an infectious smile he remembered well, and he left on that note. "Tell Erin I'll see her at lunch," he called, going out the door.

On his way back to Angie's, he stopped at the grocery store and bought ice cream. He felt they would need it to cheer them up. He held the half gallon up as he walked through the back door.

"Rockslide Brownie. How does that sound?" He slipped the ice cream into the freezer.

Her honey-brown eyes sparkled. "Decadent."

Erin raised her arms. "Oh, boy, a new flavor. Can we have it now?"

Hardy winked at his daughter and glanced at Angie. She brushed back Erin's hair. "You've been playing all morning with your friends and I want you to take a nap now. We'll have the ice cream later."

"I'm not tired. And I'm not a baby, Mama."

Angie lifted an eyebrow.

"Okay, but I'm not going to sleep."

They heard her fumbling around in her room and then

it was silence. Together they tiptoed down the hall to check on her. She was curled up on the bed, her injured leg stretched out, with her arms wrapped around the big teddy bear Hardy had given her. She was sound asleep.

They made their way back to the kitchen. Before they could sit down, they heard a knock at the front door.

Angie ran her hands down her skirt. "That must be her."

"Calm down. It's probably nothing. Or at least nothing we can't handle together."

She smiled that smile again and they both walked into the living room. Angie opened the door. A middle-aged woman with graying hair stood there, holding a briefcase.

She held out her hand. "I'm Sharon Dunlap. I spoke with you yesterday."

Angie took her hand and then opened the door wider. "I'm Angie, and this is Hardison Hollister. He's the D.A. here and also Erin's father."

"Nice to meet you, Mr. Hollister. I was unaware you would be here today." They shook hands.

"Is that a problem?"

"I would prefer to speak to Ms. Wiznowski alone." Ms. Dunlap pulled back her shoulders in a defensive stance.

"Sorry, as Erin's father, I will sit in on this discussion."

"Suit yourself."

Hardy was getting a bad feeling. Something was going on.

"Please have a seat," Angie said. He sat by Angie on the sofa, while Ms. Dunlap took a chair close to them. She opened her briefcase and took out an iPad.

"I would like to talk about your daughter's accident." Ms. Dunlap started the conversation.

"Why?" Hardy asked.

"I've received an accident report from the sheriff's

office," she stated instead of answering. "As I understand it, Erin ran out into the street and was hit by you,
Mr. Hollister."

Hardy's cell buzzed. He pulled it out of his pocket
and saw the caller ID. It was Wyatt. He stood. "I have
to take this call." He walked into the kitchen. "What is
it, Wyatt?"

"A lady from Child Protective Services has been here
asking questions. I just wanted to give you the heads-up."

"Thanks. I'll get back with you."

"Why are you asking questions about the accident?"
Angie asked as he resumed his seat.

"Because someone has filed a complaint," Hardy said.
"Am I right, Ms. Dunlap?"

"I can't divulge that kind of information."

"I'm the D.A., and I can get that information within
the hour."

Ms. Dunlap bristled. "I'm doing my job, Mr. Hollister."

"Okay. Go ahead."

Ms. Dunlap cleared her throat, looking down at the
iPad and then at Angie. "Is your daughter ever left alone?"

Angie frowned. "No. Someone is always with her."

"Yet she's ten years old and ran out into the street and
was hit. Why wasn't someone watching her?"

"Excuse me?" Angie got to her feet. Hardy caught her
hand and pulled her back down on the sofa.

"Ms. Dunlap, you have the sheriff's report." Hardy
stared directly at her. "Please read it."

"I have."

"You didn't read it correctly, then," Angie said. "It was
Erin's tenth birthday, and I gave her a party. She was having fun with her friends in the late afternoon playing on
a Slip 'N Slide in the front yard. Erin ran into the house

to get a beach ball we had bought for our trip to Disney World. The girls played with the ball for a while and then it bounced into the street. Erin ran after it. I shouted and ran after her, but she didn't hear me. I was right there. My child was not left alone at any time. The sheriff and his wife were there, as were two other parents and their children. It was an accident, just like it says in the report."

"At the time Mr. Hollister did not know he was the child's father. Am I correct?"

Angie gripped her hands in her lap, and Hardy glanced at the stark terror on her face.

PAIN SLICED THROUGH Angie, and for moment she couldn't speak. This woman was implying she was a bad mother. And she had the power to take Erin from her. Her worst fear was tearing at her heart. She quickly collected herself. Too much was at stake for her to fall apart.

"Mr. Hollister did not know Erin was his daughter at the time of the accident," she said in a clear voice.

"You withheld this information from your child?"

A steely calm came over Angie. "You do not have the right to come into my home and question my decisions."

"I do if your child is in danger."

"I assure you she is not."

Hardy got to his feet. "This conversation is over, Ms. Dunlap. And you'd better have a warrant in your hand if you want to talk to Angie or my daughter again. Someone is feeding you false information. Erin is loved and cared for."

"I would like to speak to the child."

"No way in hell."

"Mama," Erin called weakly from the doorway. Angie jumped up and went to her.

"Can we have ice cream now?" Erin looked at the

strange woman in their house and Angie had to make a decision. She had nothing to hide. She was a good mother. She believed that with all her heart. No one had a right to say that she wasn't.

"We have company," she told Erin. "Come say hello." She made the decision in an instant, and she didn't miss the puzzled look in Hardy's eyes.

Angie returned to the sofa. Erin hobbled behind her on the crutches and sat between her and Hardy. Hardy took the crutches and laid them against the sofa.

"Hi, Daddy. You stayed so we can have ice cream together?"

Hardy hugged his daughter. "You bet, peanut."

Erin looked at Ms. Dunlap again. "I'm Erin," she said.

"Nice to meet you, Erin. I'm Ms. Dunlap and—"

"Ms. Dunlap is investigating the accident," Hardy interrupted quickly.

Erin made a face. "I was a doofus."

"What do you mean?" Ms. Dunlap asked.

"I ran out into the street even after my mama told me probably a million times to always look both ways before crossing a street. I just wanted to get my ball before Mrs. Wimby saw it. If anything goes into her yard, she doesn't give it back. Mama and I were going to Disney World and I wanted my ball to play with on the beach, so I had to get it and I wasn't thinking. That's why I'm a doofus."

"Do you remember anything about the accident?"

Erin shook her head. "I just remember Mama screaming at me to stop and then I woke up in the hospital."

Ms. Dunlap tapped on the iPad. She looked up. "Do you love your mother?"

Erin smiled. "I have the best mother, but she can be mean sometimes."

Angie had no idea what her daughter was talking

about, but she let her talk because she knew Erin was her best defense.

"How can she be mean?" Ms. Dunlap inquired.

Erin leaned over and whispered, "She makes me eat healthy. Like whole-wheat bread and whole-wheat pancakes and whole-wheat waffles. Yuck. Not to mention vegetables like broccoli and asparagus, but she does put cheese on those so it's not too bad. My friend Jody and I are thinking about writing a petition and taking it to the capital in Austin to protest kids having to eat healthy meals. We should have a say in what we eat. Don't you think?"

"Uh…" Ms. Dunlap was stumped. Angie wanted to smile, but she didn't. "I'm sure she has your best interest at heart."

"Yep, that's my mama."

Ms. Dunlap studied her iPad and then asked, "Erin, does your mother ever leave you alone?"

"I can't even stay by myself while she goes to the grocery store. I have to stay with one of my aunts, my grandma or at Jody's. That's something else Jody and I were talking about. A ten-year-old should be able to stay by themselves. That's another petition we're thinking of writing. We're not babies."

"I'd listen to your mother on that one."

"I always listen to my mother, except that day when I was a doofus."

"I believe we covered that." Ms. Dunlap took a moment. "Erin, how do you feel about your father?"

"I wrote about him. Do you want to read it?"

"Uh…"

"I'll get it." Erin began to get to her feet, but Angie stopped her.

"I'll get it, sweetie." She went into Erin's room to retrieve one of the several copies of the paper that Erin had on her desk. In the living room, she handed it to Ms. Dunlap.

Hardy glanced at Angie over Erin's head, and she could see that he was as stunned by Erin responses as she was.

"Very nice," Ms. Dunlap said, laying the paper on the coffee table. "So you're not mad at your mother for keeping your father a secret from you?"

"I was for about ten seconds, but my mama loves me and I couldn't stay mad at her. And now I have my daddy."

Ms. Dunlap shoved the iPad back in her briefcase. "Thank you, Erin, for talking to me."

"Why do you have to know about the accident? Sheriff Wyatt takes care of everything in Horseshoe."

"It's just standard procedure."

"Oh."

Angie squeezed her daughter. "Why don't you get the ice cream out of the freezer and we'll have a snack?"

"Oh, boy." Erin got to her feet, and Hardy handed her the crutches.

Once Erin disappeared into the kitchen, Ms. Dunlap said, "I'll file my report and someone will be in touch with you."

Hardy stood. "I'll have that complaint on my desk by the end of the day and then I will be in touch with the head of Child Protective Services. There is no abuse or neglect in this house. Someone's going to pay for this visit, because it was totally uncalled for."

Ms. Dunlap also stood. "I'm just doing my job, Mr. Hollister."

"And I'll do mine, as her father and as the D.A. of this county. And for the record, I would've never let you talk to Erin, but Angie has made all the right decisions concerning our daughter, and I didn't question it. As you can see, Erin is a well-adjusted, happy little girl. I intend for her to stay that way."

"Good day." Ms. Dunlap walked out without another word.

Angie stared at Hardy. "This isn't over, is it?"

"I'll take care of it."

"Someone is questioning my abilities as a mother. Someone thinks I put my child in harm's way. And CPS could remove her from my custody." A chill ran through her at the mere thought, and she had to force herself to take a deep breath.

"Angie—"

"There's only one person I know who would do such a thing, and that's your father."

"I'll get to the bottom of everything, so try not to worry."

"Worry?" The sound came out as a high-pitched squeal. She took another deep breath, but it didn't stop the panic. "After she files her report, someone with CPS could knock on my door with the law, and that could very well be Wyatt, and remove Erin from my care. She would be hysterical. I would be hysterical. This is a nightmare caused by your father. I can handle a lot of things, but this isn't one of them. They can't take Erin from me. They just can't…."

Hardy took her into his arms, and his gentle touch eased the fear that was controlling her. She leaned against him, feeling his strength, his confidence. She desperately needed that right now.

He stroked her hair and she melted into his arms as if he was a wall that would hold her up no matter what happened. "Trust me. I'm going to the office and getting to the bottom of what's going on here. I'll call you later."

"Mama, Daddy, I'm eating ice cream without you," Erin called from the kitchen.

Angie stepped away and straightened her dress and her chaotic thoughts. "You have to have some ice cream or she'll know something wrong."

After eating, Hardy left. Angie glanced at the clock, knowing this would be the longest day of her life. And she prayed that Hardy could keep them from taking her child.

HARDY WENT STRAIGHT to his office and started making phone calls. The complaint had been filed in an Austin office, so he started there and as he suspected he got the runaround. But not for long.

He'd learned from the best. He'd watched his father manipulate people with the greatest of ease without them even knowing it. It took an hour and a lot of conversations, but he finally was put through to the head of Child Protective Services. From there, things began to happen.

While waiting for the man to access the records, Hardy thought about Angie. She wasn't going to have any peace until he got this settled. He wasn't, either. As long as Erin's future was at stake, he wouldn't get any rest.

Guilt knocked at his door again, and he thought he could have prevented all of this if he hadn't been so pigheaded and listened to Angie when he'd returned to Horseshoe. His daughter wouldn't have been injured and he and Angie would have found a way to raise Erin together. Even though his and Angie's lives were so different, that was the way he wanted it.

The man came back on the line and Hardy gave him his full attention. He had already faxed the accident report and letters from Wyatt, Peyton and the two other mothers who were at the scene. Hardy made sure he had all the information he needed. After he fully explained the situation and delivered a slightly veiled threat of a lawsuit, he had the name of the person who had filed the complaint. He sat in stunned silence, not wanting to believe what he was hearing. But he had to face facts. He asked for the complaint to be faxed to him, and the man agreed.

As the fax machine buzzed, anger once again filled Hardy, and he wanted to break something. He yanked the papers from the machine and headed for his truck. Hell was about to sweep across Texas.

ANGIE COULDN'T SIT still; too many troubling thoughts tortured her. She went to her office, and Erin was glad to get out of the house. But Angie couldn't concentrate there, either. On her way home she dropped kolaches off at Mrs. Hornsby's because she was having company and had asked Angie to bring them.

Once home again, the walls seemed to be closing in on her, so she called Peyton. They took glasses of lemonade out to the stoop. The girls were inside, whispering and giggling. J.W. sat in his stroller on the porch, but Angie knew that wouldn't last long. For now Dolittle was entertaining him.

The warm afternoon was like any other in Horseshoe. Most people had their sprinklers on to water their yards. Mr. and Mrs. Hillman strolled by, out for their daily exercise. They waved and Angie and Peyton waved back. The wind ruffled the leaves of the tall oaks and Dolittle took off chasing a squirrel. A typical day, but there was nothing typical about the nausea in Angie's stomach.

"I feel like running through Mrs. Wimby's sprinkler," Peyton said, fanning her face. "Are you with me?"

"No. I feel like my insides have caved in on my heart."

"Come on, Angie. No one is taking Erin from you. Hardy won't let that happen and Wyatt won't let that happen."

Angie took a sip of her lemonade. "I feel like this is my punishment for keeping Hardy away from his daughter all these years. Now they will take her away for the rest of mine. I don't know how I'm going to get through this."

"By stopping with the melodrama. They have to have solid proof before they remove a child from its home."

Angie knew that, but she just had a foreboding inside that she was about to lose everything and there was nothing she could do to stop it.

Dolittle bounded back into the yard and over to J.W. He licked the baby's face and J.W. licked him back.

"Stop that," Peyton shouted. "Do not lick the dog."

"No," J.W. shouted back.

Peyton pointed a finger at him and said, "Mommy said no."

"No," J.W. said again.

Peyton shook her head. "Gotta wonder about a kid whose first word is *no*. My blond hair is turning gray as I speak, but that's part of being a mother. We hang in there no matter what."

As Peyton said the words, Angie knew what she had to do. She got to her feet. "Could you watch Erin for about thirty minutes? I have something I need to do. It won't take long."

"Of course. Angie, please, just relax."

"I'm trying. Thanks." Angie ran into the house, placed her glass on the table, told Erin she was going out for a while and got in her car.

Peyton was right. It wasn't easy being a mother. Angie had to make things right with her own mother or she wasn't going to be able to survive the next few days. *Pride goeth before a fall.* Angie was falling, falling and she needed her mother. No matter what had happened, that fact still rang true.

Chapter Fourteen

As Angie cut through the back streets to reach her parents' house, she passed the small Catholic church she'd attended since she was a child. Her mother's car was there. She pulled into a parking spot and got out.

The parish shared a priest with three other small towns, and Father Mark was only in Horseshoe two times a week. Mr. and Mrs. Whitfield were the church caretakers and lived across the street. It was always open.

The old church was made of limestone and had stood there for over a hundred years. She opened the door and went inside. The smell of incense greeted her. She dipped her fingers into the holy water font, made the sign of the cross, genuflected and took a seat in the last wooden pew. The stained glass windows were magnificent, as was the woodwork, polished to a high sheen. The church had been well taken care of over the years.

Sitting there, a calm came over her as it always did when she entered the church. It was her happy place, where she knew her sins were forgiven and there was always hope and love. But after what she'd done, she wasn't sure she deserved forgiveness. And that was the guilt eating her up.

All this heartache could have been prevented if she'd had the courage to do what she should have when she was eighteen. That was what was killing her. She would never be able to forgive herself for what she'd done, and the only thing she knew to do was pray.

She didn't know how long she sat there just holding on to the only thing she had—her faith—when she saw her mother and Mrs. Whitfield come from the back.

Startled, her mother stared at her, and Angie thought she was going to turn away. Doris whispered something to Mrs. Whitfield and walked down the aisle to Angie.

If she ever needed her mother, she needed her now. Doris sat beside her. "I'm sorry, my baby. I'm a stubborn old woman."

That was all it took. Angie choked back a sob. "I'm sorry you're disappointed in me."

"No. No." Doris patted Angie's hands. "I couldn't face my own disappointment in myself. I should've been there for you as a mother to help you. You should have been able to come to me without fear of anger or criticism or judgment. I couldn't face what I'd done, and I didn't want to come out of my house because I saw myself as I really was—a bad mother."

Angie could hardly believe what she was hearing. Her mother was admitting she'd been wrong.

The thought gave Angie the impetus to say, "I'm scared, Mama. I've never been this scared in my whole life."

"Why?"

Angie told her what had happened.

"Who would do such a thing?" Doris shook her head. "Doesn't matter. No one is taking Erin. I will be there for you this time, and I will make sure no one hurts you again."

"Thank you, Mama. But it's out of our hands. We have to wait and see what CPS does."

"Well, I know one thing. We're going to fight this. There is no better mother than you. The whole town will testify to that."

"Hardy is looking into it."

"Then we have to trust him. Erin is his daughter, too."

Angie gripped her hands in her lap. So simple. Why couldn't she see that at eighteen?

"Sorry I didn't tell you I was pregnant with Erin. I was just so scared and—"

Her mother patted her hands again. "Shh. You were my good girl, my angel. I never worried about you getting into trouble or in with the wrong crowd. You had a good head on your shoulders, unlike your sisters. I always worried Patsy and Peggy would get pregnant before they got out of high school. Now I worry they will never get pregnant. A mother always worries."

"Back then, I loved Hardy and I didn't see what we did was wrong. I never did. It gave me Erin, and now…"

"Young love is very powerful," her mother said, surprising Angie with the insight. "I wish I could've saved you all this heartache."

Angie blinked away a tear. "Does anyone ever get this thing called life right?"

"No, but we get to say I'm sorry and move on, and that's what we do now. You're a better mother than I ever was and I defy anyone to say otherwise. Erin was right. She knows you will always be there for her. I'll always regret that I wasn't that type of mother. I'm not too old to learn, though."

Angie smiled through her glistening tears. In this church with her mother beside her, she'd gained the strength to take a step forward and to not look back, because she knew Hardy would fight for both of them.

He may not love her, but he loved his daughter. And he would not let anything or anyone harm her.

Back then, she'd wanted it all: the love, the passion, the family and the happiness beyond her wildest dreams with a man who adored her. Now she just wanted peace in her life and to know that her mistakes were forgiven—that Hardy had forgiven her.

"Come to the house and see Erin. She misses you."

"I'll follow you over and apologize to my granddaughter."

"Thank you, Mama." Arm in arm they walked out of the church into the late sunshine of the day. Maybe she and her mother could now have a better understanding of each other as mother and daughter. No matter what happened, they were family, and that was what counted most.

HARDY RANG THE doorbell, trying to control the anger shooting through him. No one came to the door. He pounded on it with his fist. After a few minutes, it was yanked open. Olivia stood in a towel, her hair dripping wet.

"Hardy, I was in the shower. I wasn't expecting you."

He pushed past her. "I bet not." He shoved the complaint papers toward her.

She ignored them. "What's wrong? No hello? No kiss?" She rubbed her hair with a towel.

"Did you really think I wouldn't find out?"

She took the papers from him, walked into the living room and set them on the coffee table. "What do you want me to say?"

"I want you to tell me why you would do such a thing. You met with someone in the CPS office and said you were the attorney for Hardison Hollister Sr. You claimed because of the accident he was concerned about the safety and welfare of his granddaughter. On that complaint alone, they looked into your allegations. False allegations. You used my father's name without his permission. That's a criminal act."

"How do you know your father didn't instruct me to intervene?"

"Because I asked him point-blank, and if there's anything consistent about my father, it's that he finds it hard to lie when asked a direct question. It must be something to do with being a judge. It's like he's on the witness stand. He will not lie."

She turned to face him, anger marring the beautiful lines of her face. "I did it for us. You were spending all your time with her and the kid. I put a solid year into our relationship, and you were throwing it all away because you found out you were a father. You stopped thinking about the campaign. All you thought about was the kid. Even your father could see your career was going down the tubes."

"My career is my business."

"I have supported you and promoted you whenever I could, so don't tell me it's none of my business."

He took a deep breath to marshal his thoughts. "What did you hope to gain by this?" He pointed to the papers.

"I was trying to save your future—our future."

"How could taking my daughter from her mother save our future?"

"You would see that that country small-town girl was not the woman for you. She would bring you down instead of lifting you up."

"I'm not following you. All I see is a bitter woman reacting out of jealousy. You were afraid you were going to lose me to Angie, so you did your damnedest to stop it."

"Do you really think she'll fit into your lifestyle? Do

you honestly see her socializing with judges, congress-men and senators? And her family? That's a whole other matter. They're a bunch of rednecks and would be an embarrassment to you. Yet you're willing to ruin your life for her."

Something in Olivia's words resonated with him. He tried to push it away, but there it was, hidden in the dark-est crevices of his mind. *Oh, God!* Guilt wasn't the reason he'd never called Angie. It was something else entirely, and at that moment he hated himself.

Olivia saw the chink in his armor. "Hardy, you do know what I'm talking about, don't you? I'm not trying to be mean or insulting. I'm sure Angie's a very nice per-son, but she's not the woman for you."

"You know nothing about Angie. She's warm and lov-ing. Someone you could never be. Stay away from me and Angie and our daughter. If you go anywhere near them, I will file charges against you. Just stay out of my life."

"You don't mean that."

"I do."

"I just wanted to scare her so she would get out of your life and stop making you feel guilty over your daughter."

"You achieved your goal. Angie is scared out of her mind, and for that I will never forgive you."

"She will bore you to death in two months."

"I spent so many years trying to be what my father wanted me to be, and now I don't even know who I am. I feel used and disillusioned." He quickly collected him-self and picked up her portable phone. Handing it to her, he said, "Call CPS and tell them the complaint was a lie fabricated by you."

She stiffened. "Why would I do that?"

"Because you falsely used my father's name, and I will

file charges against you so fast it will make your head spin. Are you willing to risk your law career?"

"Hardy." She moved closer to him.

He stared at her. "Don't embarrass yourself."

She made the call.

Hardy strolled toward the door.

"Hardy."

He stopped.

"You'll never realize your dream with her."

He opened the door and walked to his truck, feeling as low as he'd ever felt. Once inside, he called CPS. After a short discussion, Hardy agreed not to file charges against CPS and not to alert the media. In return, the man pulled the complaint and erased it from the system.

He then punched in Angie's number. He couldn't let her worry any longer.

"I just wanted to let you know that the complaint is being dropped. No one is taking Erin. It won't even be on the record."

"Oh, Hardy, thank you. I can breathe again." He could hear the relief in her voice, and for a moment he just held the phone close to his ear. *Forgive me* echoed through his mind. "Who filed the complaint, and how did you get it dropped?"

"I'll tell you when I get back to Horseshoe. I just didn't want you to worry anymore. Is Erin okay?"

"Yes, she's on the porch with Jody."

"I'll talk to you later."

He clicked off and drove out of the parking area, wondering how he was going to tell Angie what he had to.

Chapter Fifteen

Angie saw the lights turn into her driveway. She ran to the back door. It was dark, but she knew it was Hardy. She'd been waiting and waiting. Where had he been, and why wasn't he getting out of his truck? After a moment, a dark figure walked toward the door. She quickly opened it.

Hardy's haggard appearance startled her. His dark hair was tousled as if he'd been running his fingers through it repeatedly. His pristine white shirt was wrinkled and a frown marred his handsome face. He brought the warmth of the night in with him, but her heart felt cold because she knew what he had to tell her wasn't going to be good.

"May I see Erin?"

"Sure."

She followed him down the hall into Erin's room. He sat on the bed and brushed Erin's hair from her face. Leaning over, he kissed her forehead.

"Daddy," Erin whispered sleepily.

"Night, sleeping beauty."

"Night."

He got up and they went back into the kitchen.

"Do you have any coffee?" he asked.

She looked at the clock on the wall. "It's almost ten."

"You're right. I'm wired enough."

She opened the refrigerator. "I made lemonade today. How about a glass?"

"Do you have some vodka to put in it?" He pulled out a chair and took a seat.

"No." She opened the refrigerator and removed the lemonade. Pouring two glasses, she asked, "That bad, huh?"

He ran his hands up his face. "A day I don't want to relive."

After placing the glasses on the table, she sat across from him. "What happened? Who filed the complaint?"

"Olivia."

"What? Why would she do that?"

He told her the whole story.

"You're positive your father had nothing to do with it?"

He nodded. "Yes."

"I don't know what to say. *Bitch* comes to mind, but I know you cared about her. I'm sorry it turned out this way."

He twisted the glass. "It's over, so don't worry about losing Erin. No one can take her from you."

"Thank you."

He ran his finger over the wetness of the glass. "I've been driving around trying to figure out a way to tell you something that I realized tonight for the first time. Or at least I allowed myself to realize it."

Her breath stalled, and she wanted to say she didn't need to know anything else, but that was a coward's way out. She had to hear what he had to say.

"You were right. That summer long ago I fell in love, and I denied it every way I could for a reason." He took a gulp of the lemonade as if it was pure vodka. "You see, my father had this future planned for me and I didn't see you as someone to share that future with. You were young and…"

When he didn't say anything else, she finished the sentence. "I wasn't the type of woman you saw as your wife."

"Yeah. I can't believe I was that shallow. I don't feel that way now—please, believe me." Before she could find a response, he went on, "That's why when you tried to talk to me when I first came back, I avoided you. I didn't want to reopen that door to old feelings, and I didn't want to hurt your feelings. I only saw you as an obstacle to the future I had planned. You derailed me once, and I couldn't let it happen again. Don't feel bad about not getting in touch with me ten years ago. I probably wouldn't have taken your call. So it's all on me, Angie. Don't ever blame yourself again."

As he talked, a thread of pain wrapped around her heart. The more he talked, the more the thread tightened. But she would not give in to it. She would not creep away and bawl her eyes out. She'd always known she would never fit into his world.

"I've always felt I wasn't good enough for you, but it was hard to tell my heart that."

His gaze shot to hers. "Don't say that. Coming here in the past few weeks, watching you with Erin and with your family and with your friends, I could see everything I couldn't back then. I saw a loving, caring, compassionate woman who any man would be lucky to have."

She got up and carried her glass to the sink. She turned to face him, leaning against the counter for support. "I think that now we have to forgive each other and move forward. We could blame each other forever and it would solve nothing. We had a wonderful summer that year and I would like to look back on it with fondness because we created Erin. What happened afterward was two people who had no clue of what they really wanted. At the time, they just wanted each other."

His tortured eyes looked into hers. "Angie, I'd like to start over."

She shook her head. "There's no going back, Hardy. I'm a homebody. I love being a mother and I love cooking and taking care of my yard and my flowers. I have a lot of customers who depend on me, and I enjoy helping them and anyone who needs my help. That's who I am. I'm not cut out to be a politician's wife. I wasn't then, and I'm not now. I'd hate going to parties, campaigning, asking for votes and generally just being out there. I'd much rather be at home. That makes me sound really old, but…"

He got up and walked to her. He cupped her face with his hands. She tensed. With his thumb, he caressed her cheek. "I'm sorry I hurt you. You're the sweetest person I know and I wish I could go back and—"

"We can't. As adults, we have to think of Erin and do what's best for her. She will live with me and you can see her whenever you want. I hope we can make better choices for her together without arguing and without antagonism. If anything, we've grown from this."

"Why do you have to be so nice? I wish you would yell at me, curse me or something."

She placed her hands over his and entwined her fingers with his. "Please, just go." She didn't know how much more strength she had, and she was getting close to the breaking point.

"Goodbye, Angie." With those words, he let go of her hands and walked out the door. Any dreams she'd harbored were gone. A tear ran down her cheek for a love that wasn't meant to be.

HARDY DIDN'T SLEEP much that night. His conscience wouldn't let him. He'd hurt the most loving person on earth, and for that he couldn't forgive himself. But he would go on. That was what life was about.

By morning he'd made a decision. His father wasn't at the breakfast table, so he turned to Mavis. "Where's Dad?"

"He's on the phone upstairs. I heard him when I was gathering laundry. I'm sure it's some political strategy for your future."

His father walked into the room, and Mavis handed him a cup coffee. "I called Olivia and she said I needed to talk to you. Did you break up with her?"

"Yes."

"Hot damn. Now we're talking." As soon as the words left Mavis's mouth, she clamped a hand over it.

Hardison Senior glared at her as he took a seat. "Don't you have something to do in another part of the house?"

"Yes, sir. I have to clean the stinky cigars out of your study." Mavis had been with them so long she had no qualms about voicing her opinion.

As soon as she left, his dad asked, "What happened?"

Hardy told his father everything about the day before.

"She used my name?"

"Yes, that's why CPS looked into the complaint."

"I never thought she'd go that far, but she saw what everyone else saw."

"What?"

"That you're smitten with your daughter…and the daughter's mother."

Hardy got up and placed his cup on the counter. "I'm not sure what the next step is, Dad. I want you to know that. Don't push me. Don't pressure me. This time I'm making a decision that's for me—a decision for my future."

"I kind of figured that. Take your time. You may not believe it, but I really do want you to be happy. But don't think I'm giving up, either."

Hardy was stunned for a second. He expected an argument—a big argument. He'd finally gotten through to his dad, and it was a relief. "Thanks. I wish Rachel was here. I really need to talk to her."

"She's not answering her phone again. She's mad at me because I gave her a good talking-to the last time. I don't know why she can't come home. It's as if she hates it here, and I know that's not true." He got up to refill his cup. "Kids will drive you crazy."

"At the moment, mine only brings me joy."

"You wait until she hits those teen years. You won't even recognize her. Which reminds me. When are you bringing Erin to the house?"

"I'm not sure, but you can visit her at Angie's. Just call."

Hardy headed for his truck and the office. On the way, he called Erin. She was up and eating breakfast and actually answered the phone. Angie was putting clothes in the washer, Erin said. They talked until he reached the courthouse. His daughter was a chatterbox.

Alice was at her desk. He took his messages from her. "Wyatt's looking for you."

"Thanks. I'll call him." He walked into his office, sorting his messages. Wyatt came in behind him.

"I got word a little while ago that Nelda Cleck's five-year-old son passed away."

"Oh, man!" Hardy sank into his chair. Nelda's boyfriend had beaten the boy into a coma two weeks ago. Hardy had really hoped the kid would pull through.

"The boyfriend's out on bail," Wyatt said. "What do you want me to do?"

"I'll upgrade the charges, and you can pick him up. He's going to do some hard time now."

Wyatt shook his head. "I don't know what makes a man do something like that."

"Too much liquor, for one thing." Hardy leaned forward. "Nelda lives in a two-bedroom trailer and has five more kids. I don't know where they all sleep. At least we can get the boyfriend out of there."

"We're getting a bad environment in that trailer park. Don't forget the meeting tonight with the mayor and the city council. They want us to keep crime down, but they're gonna have to set some restrictions. Like how many people in a trailer and how many trailers on a lot. We patrol that area all the time, but we need some help from the city to stop the influx of hoods moving in."

"What time is the meeting?"

"Seven."

Wyatt moved for the door. "Call me when you have the paperwork ready."

Crimes like the Cleck case got to Hardy. He stood and went to the window. He had a corner office and could see most of Horseshoe. Angie drove up and parked in front of her office. She must not be staying long because she usually parked around back. He watched as if mesmerized as she got the crutches out of the car and carried them around to Erin in the passenger side. Angie waited until Erin hopped up onto the curb and then retrieved a box out of the backseat. It looked like folders and her laptop. Before she could unlock her door, Mr. Zapota and Mrs. Whitfield stopped to chat. His daughter was doing most of the chatting. He could almost hear her voice.

Mrs. Watkins from the antiques store walked up.

Angie was having a hard time getting into her office. Finally, AnaMarie opened the door from the inside and Angie and Erin were able to escape from the people who wanted to talk to them. He didn't know why Angie thought she wasn't a social person. Everyone liked her and enjoyed her company.

In that moment as he watched, something happened inside him. He wanted to run from his office down the steps of the courthouse and to Angie and Erin. They were everything he wanted. Nothing else mattered. They were his future. His present and his past. He took a deep breath, knowing that this time he had to take it slow so Angie would know that he really wanted her. Loved her. How did he do that?

ANGIE TRIED NOT to think of the conversation with Hardy, but most of the time it was right there at the edge of her consciousness. But she tried not to let it get to her. They would see each other often, so she had to be able to talk to him without any hurt feelings. Sometimes it was hard to let go of the dream. That was why she wouldn't have a relationship with Hardy. She wanted him to have *his* dream. Soon he would realize it was for the best. He would make a great judge, and she had a feeling he would pursue politics at an even higher level.

The day was busy. Erin was doing fine, entertaining everyone who came into the bakery or Angie's office. Angie went to the grocery store on the way home and wondered if Hardy would come by tonight. She had to stop thinking about him.

"It's not fair!" Erin complained from the living room.

Angie put milk and orange juice into the refrigerator. "Erin, I'm getting tired of this."

Someone tapped at the back door.

"Come in."

Hardy stepped into her kitchen and her heart beat a little faster just at the sight of him. Was it always going to be that way?

"Where's Erin?" he asked.

"In the living room pouting."

"I'm not pouting," Erin shouted. "I'm mad."

"What's going on?" Hardy wanted to know.

"The Fourth of July picnic and parade is a few days away and she's just realized she won't be able to ride her bicycle in the parade with Jody like she always does. They decorate the bikes in red, white and blue. They've done it every year since they were about five."

Hardy walked into the living room. Angie continued to put up the groceries, but she had one ear tuned to everything that was being said in the other room.

"It's not fair, Daddy," Erin said. "I have to sit and watch."

"You know, I have a red convertible Camaro I used to drive in college. It's in the garage at the ranch. I'll see if I can get it running, and then you can ride in the parade. You can sit in the back and wave like a beauty queen."

"Can Jody ride, too?"

"If her parents say it's okay."

"Ah, Mama, did you hear?" Erin's voice was now filled with excitement.

"Yes, I heard," Angie said from the doorway. She remembered the car. Hardy had looked like a movie star driving it. Well, to her innocent eyes, he had.

Hardy got to his feet. "I'll go home and see if it still runs."

"I'll call Uncle Bubba." Erin reached for her crutches. "He fixes a lot of old cars."

"Now, you know your uncle and I don't get along that well."

"Don't worry," was Erin's response. "I'll talk to him, and he'll do anything for me."

She hobbled into the kitchen for the phone.

Angie lifted an eyebrow at Hardy. "Mr. Fix-It?"

He stepped closer to her and her breath caught in her throat at the gleam in his eyes. "That's me. Got anything you want me to fix?"

My heart.

"Daddy, Uncle Bubba wants to talk to you," Erin called.

Hardy grinned. "See. It's working."

BUBBA HAULED THE Camaro to his station and had it running the next day. Erin was beside herself with anticipation. Bubba even washed it and cleaned it up. Angie expected a phone call at any minute that Bubba had whacked Hardy over the head with a wrench, but it seemed the D.A. had won over her brother.

Angie and Peyton took the girls to a mall in Temple to get outfits for the parade. Hardy gave her his credit card to buy whatever Erin wanted. At first she refused, but then she relented and took the card. Erin was his daughter, too. She had to remind herself every now and then.

The girls settled on red cowboy boots, white skirts, blue T-shirts with The Fourth of July written on them, a red sash for their waists and white hats. The day of the parade Erin could hardly contain herself. Hardy picked Erin up early and Angie was surprised to see Judge Hollister sitting in the passenger seat. Hardy helped Erin into the small backseat and then waved to Angie.

As they drove away, Angie felt a pang. She didn't know what it was at first, and then it hit her. It was the first step of letting go and sharing Erin with her father. She went into the house, feeling lonelier than she ever had. She didn't have time to have a meltdown because she and Peyton were in charge of drinks and popcorn.

The festive day passed quickly, as most of Horseshoe was there to celebrate. Angie held her breath as she waited for the line of cars and makeshift floats to make the trip around the square. She kept looking for the red Camaro and when she saw it, she had to fight not to cry.

Erin and Jody sat side by side on the back of the Camaro just like beauty queens, waving. Judge Hollister waved to the crowd, also. It was a defining moment, and everyone in Horseshoe knew it. The Hollisters were introducing Erin as part of the family.

The whole Wiznowski family was manning a kolache booth. All the grandmothers were there, including Helen and Ruby. Five generations were present. Later they would take a photo to commemorate the occasion.

The square was a hive of activity. People were barbecuing, selling hot dogs and hamburgers, drinks, cotton candy, hot pretzels, funnel cakes and much more. Patsy and Peggy were face painting. There was a forty-two-domino tournament and games for the kids to play. Country music played in the background.

Angie and Peyton sold drinks and popcorn and never had a moment's break. It was hot and people were thirsty. There were several booths sponsored by the city, and all proceeds went to the Horseshoe school district to fund a swimming pool for the kids. Last year they'd made enough to renovate the gym.

As Angie filled cups with ice and soft drinks or water, she kept looking for Erin. She wanted to make sure Erin wasn't getting too much sun, but she was sure Hardy would take care of her. She just didn't like being away from her daughter.

At lunchtime, she went searching for Erin. She had to be tired by now standing on the crutches. Angie found her with Jody by the Camaro with Hardy, the judge and several members of the city council. They were discussing the trailer park and the Cleck child who had died. It was a sad situation.

She walked over to Erin and Jody. "Sweetie, come get something to drink and eat. It's too hot out here for you, and I want you to sit down for a while."

"Mama, I'm with Daddy," Erin said in a voice that denoted Angie was embarrassing her.

Erin had never spoken to her that way, and it took a moment to gain her perspective.

Hardy walked over. "Erin, go with your mother."

Erin hung her head. "Yes, sir."

Angie found a spot under a huge oak tree and made Erin sit down in the shade. Her cheeks were red from the heat and her T-shirt was sweaty.

Peyton brought plates of hot dogs, chips and cookies for the girls and also one for Angie. Erin drank almost a bottle of water and then she lay on the grass with her head in Angie's lap. Her daughter was unwilling to admit she was tired. She just wanted to spend time with her father and Angie had to try to adjust.

The afternoon passed quickly. A small band was setting up on the courthouse steps. The booths started to close, and everyone gathered for the evening's entertainment. Erin and Jody sat in lawn chairs by the paved entrance to the courthouse where people would dance.

Wyatt and his guys had to work because there was a lot of drinking during the picnic, which made some people rowdy, but he came over for the dance and Peyton was thrilled. J.W. went home with his grandmother, and Angie and Peyton found seats near the girls. Hardy and Wyatt stood behind them. When the music started, Wyatt and Peyton were the first to get up. Then Wyatt danced with Jody.

"I want to dance with my daddy," Erin whined.

"Sweetie, you can't. Maybe next year. You're getting tired and cranky and I want the whining to stop. You've had a big day."

Erin leaned over into Angie's lap. "I'm sorry, Mama. Can we go home now?"

Before Angie could reply, Hardy walked up to Erin. "Stand up," he instructed. Erin did as he asked. "Now put your arms around my neck." He leaned forward and Erin once again did as asked. Hardy lifted Erin from the lawn chair into his arms. With his arms around her waist, they moved to the music playing in the background. The smile on Erin's face said it all. Angie felt a catch in her throat.

After the song died away, Hardy brought Erin back and sat her in her chair.

"Now you have to dance with Mama." Erin pointed to Angie.

Angie shook her head. "No. I'm too tired."

Hardy reached for her hand and pulled her to her feet. She had no choice other than to make a fool of herself or dance. She danced. He pulled her against his firm body and clasped his hands at the small of her back. Her lungs burned from holding her breath at the sweet desire that ran through her.

Wrapping her arms around his neck, she went with her emotions. The side of his face rested against her forehead. His five-o'clock shadow felt wicked against her skin. The band played on as the moonlight cast its magic spell. Hardy smelled of barbecue, cigars and heaven. Yes, heaven had a scent, and it flooded her system with an aching need.

Hardy pulled her closer and she was aware of every inch of his masculine body. Her hands entwined in his hair at his nape. She was spellbound. She should step away, but she wanted something she found hard to deny.

"This is nice," Hardy whispered. "This is right."

Words clogged in her throat, and she didn't respond. She was glad when the George Strait song ended. But Hardy didn't release her and the band broke into "If Tomorrow Never Comes" by Garth Brooks, and Angie's heart squeezed with anguish. What if Hardy never knew how much she loved him? *What difference would that make?* the cynic in her replied.

Angie was glad when the song ended. She hurried back to her daughter. The band played "Boot Scootin' Boogie" and the younger folks took over the dancing.

Erin was half-asleep. Hardy carried her to the Camaro and drove her home. Angie packed up her stuff, said goodbye to Peyton and followed them. She unlocked the door and Hardy carried Erin to her bedroom.

"I can walk," Erin complained.

"You're half-asleep and I'm afraid you'll trip," Hardy told her.

Hardy laid Erin on the bed and kissed her cheek. "Good night, sleeping beauty."

"I had a good time, Daddy. Thank you."

"You're welcome."

"I love you, Daddy."

Angie stood next to Hardy, and he tensed. It was the first time Erin had said the words without them being a response to Hardy's *I love you.* She wanted to say something, but she waited for him because it was his moment.

"I love you, too. More than I can ever tell you." His voice was hoarse.

"We're cool, huh?"

"So cool." He kissed her one more time and walked out of the room.

Angie hurriedly undressed Erin because she was dozing off even as she worked with her. She pulled a T-shirt over Erin's head and tucked her in. She was out for the night.

The moon was full and Angie hadn't turned on any lights when they had come in. She walked into the kitchen and jumped as she saw a figure by the sink. She let out a deep breath when she saw it was Hardy.

"I thought you had gone."

"Let's get married. I want us to be a family."

Angie sighed. "Hardy, we've been through this."

"Don't you want to make a home for Erin?"

"I have made a home for Erin."

"But I'm not in it." His words were sharp. Angie held her tongue because they were both tired and she didn't want to say anything she'd regret tomorrow.

"I thought we decided to do away with the guilt card. Just because Erin said she loved you is not a reason for us to get married."

"It's more than that and you know it. When we were dancing tonight, you felt it and I felt it. We belong together. Those old emotions are still there."

"Hardy…" She didn't know what else to say.

"How do you know you won't make a politician's wife? You're a social person. Every time you go out, people gravitate toward you. They want to talk to you and you respond in kind. And I never said I don't enjoy being at home. I can help with Erin, the yard and the house. You just have to give us a chance."

She bit her lip and gauged her next words. "We're two very different people and we want different things out of life. In six months you'll feel differently. In a year you'll know that I'm right. In two years you'll thank me for not keeping you from pursuing your dreams."

Stepping closer to her, he tucked stray strands of curls behind her ear. Her body trembled. "Dreams change, Angie."

She shook her head. "I don't want to be the reason for your dreams to change, because years down the road you'll blame me. It's time for us to go our separate ways. Our time has passed."

He stepped away. "I know what I want in my heart. It has taken me eleven years to figure that out. Now it's time for you to figure out what you want because I'm not changing my mind. The next move is yours." He walked out the door.

She stood in the kitchen with tears rolling down her cheeks.

When would the heartache be over?

Chapter Sixteen

Life settled into a routine and Angie and Hardy treated each other cordially. He talked about child support. She refused to listen. To keep from the disagreement turning into a full-blown argument, Hardy set up an account for Erin with Angie as signee. The money was there if Erin ever needed it. Angie didn't fight it. She knew taking responsibility for his child was important to him.

Hardy was at the house every day after work and Angie made a point of leaving so he could spend time with Erin. It worked better for her that way. Hardy didn't say anything. As he said, the next move was up to her.

They went to Temple to see the doctor for Erin. The doctor deemed her healed, and she walked out without her crutches. Their daughter couldn't stop giggling. The doctor only asked that she take it easy and not do anything really strenuous for a while. Erin was excited to be on her own again.

Angie and Peyton decided to take the girls to Six Flags Over Texas at Arlington so they could have some fun for the summer.

The girls had a fabulous time, especially since they stayed in a hotel that had a pool. Angie and Peyton even rode some of the rides and the girls laughed at them. It was a vacation about pure fun. On the way home, they stopped at a mall and shopped for school clothes. They were sunburned and happy when they pulled into Angie's driveway. Peyton and Jody waved goodbye and headed home to J.W. and Wyatt.

Erin had talked to Hardy several times, telling him everything she was doing, and she called as soon as they entered the house. Angie went to unpack. The vacation had been good for her. Her perspective was changing and she wasn't clinging so hard to the guilt.

School started, and Hardy arrived to take Erin on her first day. It was a frenzied morning of "what to wear?" Finally, Angie picked out an outfit and made her daughter keep it on. She modeled it for Hardy.

His eyes caught hers over Erin's head. "Beautiful," he said, and she had the insane thought he was talking about her. She quickly brushed it away.

With school back in session, their days fell into a routine. Hardy took Erin to school and Angie picked her up. They spoke very little and Angie missed spending time with him. She missed him.

AS DAYS TURNED into weeks, Angie showed no signs of changing their relationship. Hardy decided not to run for judge. His dad just shook his head and walked away. The judge was spending a lot of time in Austin with his lady friend, and Hardy was grateful for the diversion. He knew his dad hadn't given up on him, but Hardy was in control of his life now, or more to the point, Angie was. He had a feeling he was going to spend the rest of his life watching her out of his window.

At the end of October, Hardy realized the holidays were drawing near and he wanted to spend them with Angie and Erin. The ranch was lonely with no one there. As the days continued to pass, the loneliness became part of him. But he'd wait forever if he had to. Until she believed that he loved her.

THE BAKERY WAS busy as the people of Horseshoe grabbed something before heading to work. Last year they'd bought the building next door and expanded the bakery and made a bigger office for Angie. She had a private entrance, and she liked it that way.

The scent of vanilla and apples greeted her as she entered her office. *Oh, yeah.* The smell of the bakery was pure heaven. She'd brightened her office with terra-cotta walls and ivy and a ficus plant. Since it was Friday, she turned on her computer and settled in to make out the payroll.

"Is Erin in school?" Her mother walked in with a big apron covering her dress and a hairnet over her hair.

"Of course."

"You used to bring her to the bakery so we could see her before she left for the day."

"Her father takes her to school now."

"Oh, yeah. Mr. Hollister." Doris tapped Angie on the shoulder. "I have to admit that Mr. Hollister is a good father. When are you going to marry him? You need to be a real family. Erin deserves that."

Angie gritted her teeth and was prevented from answering by AnaMarie entering the room.

"Mama, I need you in the kitchen. We have a big order to get out for the volunteer fire department and the Lions Club in Temple."

"I'm coming."

AnaMarie arched an eyebrow. "Saved you. You owe me."

"You name it."

AnaMarie chuckled and went back to the kitchen.

Before Angie could get back to work, Peyton came into her office from the bakery. J.W. was in his stroller, munching on a tea cake.

Peyton sank into a chair across from Angie's desk. "I'm taking kolaches over to Wyatt and Stuart and thought I'd say hello. How are things going?"

"Good." Angie knelt down to kiss the baby, and he pointed a finger covered with cake at her. "He gets more adorable every day."

"Of course he does. He takes after his mother."

Angie laughed and resumed her seat. Doubts and insecurities kept taunting her. She looked at her friend, needing answers.

"When you left Horseshoe, what made you come back? How did you know that you wanted to live here instead of your old life in Austin?"

Peyton flipped back her long blond hair. "I must say it was an experience to get arrested and spend time in jail for a spoiled, pampered rich girl. It was the best thing that happened to me, though. I woke up and saw that the world didn't owe me a thing. I grew up. When I went back to Austin, I wasn't the same person. I left my heart in Horseshoe—with Wyatt."

"I know. You told me that, but what I'm asking is what gave you the courage to come back even after Wyatt told you it was over."

"It was simple. I was miserable without him, so I came back with my heart in my hand. I took a risk. That's what love is. You have to take a risk. If it's real, it's not a risk it all." Peyton reached over and gave the baby a piece of tea cake he'd dropped on the stroller tray. "Tell me about Hardy."

Angie moved the papers around on her desk. "He wants us to get married and—"

"What are you waiting for?"

"Love. Real love. I want him to love me more than anything on this earth. I don't want him to marry me because of Erin."

"Angie, open your eyes. The man is at your house every day. He'd do anything you asked. Everybody can see the way he feels about you—why can't you?" Peyton held up a hand. "Please don't tell me you're not good enough or not pretty enough or I might jump across this desk and smack you."

Angie laughed in spite of herself. Peyton could always cheer her up. "I've made so many mistakes."

"Oh, please. Like no one ever makes mistakes. If you love Hardy, you'd better do something about it. No." Peyton shook her head. "I know you love him. You've never stopped, even though you won't admit it. So get your butt over to the courthouse and tell him that. For heaven's sakes, it's time for a little happiness. Take a risk."

Long after Peyton had left, Angie thought about what she'd said. She wasn't ever going to get over him, so she had to have the courage to tell him how she felt. Maybe…

She grabbed her purse, locked her office and walked across the street. Today she was taking a risk.

ON THE WAY over, she reminded herself that nothing had changed. Hardy hadn't once said that he loved her. Maybe she wouldn't get the whole fantasy, but she knew one thing: she loved him and couldn't live without him. If that made her weak, then so be it. She wanted her family together—the three of them.

People who worked at the courthouse were leaving for the day. She spoke to several as she went inside. The place smelled of old paper, dust and time, which she realized didn't have a smell. It was more of a feeling that she was walking in places where so many other people had walked before.

She took the stairs up to the second floor where the D.A.'s office was located. Alice was standing at her desk, getting ready to leave.

"Oh, Angie, you startled me. I wasn't expecting anyone."

"Is Hardy in?"

She glanced nervously toward Hardy's closed door, and Angie thought for a moment that maybe he was with someone.

"Yes, but…"

"But what?"

"He's not in a good mood."

"Don't worry. I'm not, either." She walked toward the door and placed her hand on the knob. Taking a deep breath, she turned it and went inside.

Hardy sat at his desk. His sleeves were rolled up to the elbows and his hair was mussed, but what caught her attention were the worry lines on his face.

He got up the moment he saw her. "Angie, something wrong? Where's Erin?"

"Today is dance day. Peyton took the girls."

"I forgot." He seemed to relax.

She gave the room a quick glance. It was the first time she'd been in his office, and it was larger than she'd expected. It was paneled in dark wood, and he had a huge mahogany desk with two leather chairs in front of it. A brown leather sofa occupied one wall with end tables and lamps with horse sculptures as the base. A laptop, papers and folders were on his desk. Her eyes froze on one item: a picture.

There amid his work was a photo of her and Erin. She couldn't tear her eyes away.

He came around the desk. "Are you okay? You've never been to my office before."

"Yes." Her eyes strayed back to the picture. "Where did you get that?"

"I took it with my phone. The guy in the photo shop at the pharmacy made them for me." He motioned to another wall. "I picked out the best, and the guy touched them up." There were more photos of Erin. Angie was at a complete loss, and words stuck in her mouth like scratchy wool. She was there for a reason and for a moment she couldn't remember what it was.

It was understandable for him to have pictures of Erin. But he had a picture of her. That had her speechless and giddy all at the same time. She wasn't sure whether to laugh or cry, and she knew this was a defining moment for her.

Before she could find the right words, he said, "I was talking to Wyatt, and he's thinking of taking Jody to the football game tonight. I thought I'd take Erin, too, if that's okay with you?"

"Uh…sure."

"It's been a hell of a day and I could use a distraction."

"What's going on?"

"CPS took Nelda Cleck's five other children and she's trying to get them back. Her lawyer was just here and wanted me to put in a good word for her. I told her the D.A.'s office had little to do with that, but I would make sure that Nelda's home life was investigated thoroughly. The children are not going back into an abusive home. Nelda needs to understand her children come first."

He was clearly upset with the situation and she couldn't blame him. Not for the first time, she realized how stressful his job was.

He ran his hands through his already tousled hair.

"People somehow don't understand the value of a life. The lawyer had the gall to even ask me to go easy on the boyfriend, saying Nelda assured her he didn't mean to hurt the little boy. It was an accident and she pleaded for me to reduce the charge to involuntary manslaughter. I told her the murder charge stands. She left in a snit."

She could feel his pain. Even in a small town like Horseshoe, there were still heinous crimes. "I'm sorry," was all she could say.

"I just keep thinking about that day I hit Erin with my truck. She could've died. I could've killed my own child, and I'd be no better than the boyfriend."

"Don't say that. Erin is fine. Stop doing this to yourself."

He gave a deep sigh. "It's been a long day. I'm looking forward to getting out of the office and spending some time with my daughter." He shuffled some papers into a folder. "Is there a reason you came by?"

"Uh…it can wait." This wasn't the time to declare her love or talk about the future. And she was beginning to wonder if there ever would be.

"Erin gets home about six from dance, right?"

"Yes."

"I'll pick her up about six-thirty."

Angie moved toward the door. With her hand on the knob, she stopped. She was taking the easy way out, like always. This was her future, and she'd told herself a million times she would make better decisions. She took a deep breath and turned back.

She cleared her throat. "There is a reason I stopped by."

He looked up and at his tired eyes her courage sank to the bottom of her stomach.

"Uh…you said the next move would be up to me." The

brightening of his eyes rescued her courage and bolstered her resolve. "I wanted to tell you…that…I love you."

"What?" He stood so fast his chair went flying backward. "Does this mean…?"

"Yes. It means I will marry you."

He frowned. "For Erin?"

She shook her head. "You and Erin have a good relationship. I don't need to marry you for that. I love you. I've loved you since I was eighteen years old, and I think it's about time to admit that and to start our life together."

He came around the desk and stood about a foot from her, staring into her eyes. "Say that again."

"I love you."

He gathered her into his arms and kissed her. All her doubts and insecurities disappeared. She kissed him back with all the fervor of her unrequited love.

"I love you, too," he whispered against her mouth, and then he just held her, rocking her gently from side to side. "Now…you were saying something about marriage."

She reached up and kissed his neck. "Yes, I'm ready to take that leap."

"You're not worried about being a politician's wife?"

She rested her head in the curve of his neck. "A little, but I think I can handle it as long as you love me."

"I love you. We've wasted too many years and I don't want to waste one more minute."

She squealed, threw her arms around his neck and met his kiss with excitement, desire and passion. Gently moving her around, he fell backward onto the sofa, his lips never leaving hers. He pulled her down, and they lay entwined, heart against heart, their bodies melting together. Oh, yeah, this was what she wanted. All of him. Forever.

A long time later, he got up and went to his desk. He

came back with a jewelry box. She sat up, brushing her hair away from her face.

"Oh." She looked into his smoldering eyes. "You bought a ring?"

"I was just waiting for you to make up your mind because I wasn't going anywhere. I'm not going anywhere without you ever again." He opened the box, and the most gorgeous diamond sparkled as brightly as the hope in his eyes. She held her breath as he slipped it onto her finger. Tears ran down her cheeks and she didn't know why. She was happy.

He lifted her into his arms and kissed her deeply. The kiss went on and on until an annoying tap at the door interrupted.

"I'm going home, Hardy," Alice called through the door. "Do you need anything else?"

He gave Angie a quick kiss. "I have everything I need."

"Whatever," they could hear Alice mumble.

They laughed. Angie had never felt so happy in her life. As his lips found hers again, her cell buzzed.

"Damn," Hardy said.

"I have to get it." Angie eased away. "It might be our daughter."

She found her purse on the floor where she'd dropped it. It was Erin. Angie held her hand over the phone. "She wants to know if she can go to the football game with Jody tonight."

Hardy gave a thumbs-up with a wicked grin.

Slipping the phone back into her purse, she asked, "Are you sure you don't want to take her to the game?"

He took her into his arms again. "Daddy has other plans. I know our daughter will understand it's Mama and Daddy time." He kissed the side of her face. "Let's continue this at home where we can lock doors, get naked and enjoy wild sex to our heart's content."

She giggled, feeling like a schoolgirl. She buttoned his shirt and straightened her blouse with a smile on her face. They walked out of the courthouse arm in arm to start the rest of their lives.

Epilogue

One year later...

To Angie Hollister, the sweetest sound in the world was Hardy's and their daughter's laughter.

She paused and listened to their antics. Soon Hardy strolled into their bedroom.

"What's all the laughter about?" she asked, zipping her suitcase.

"I helped Erin close her case and lifted it to the floor. It was so heavy I told her I'd better check to see if she had Jody in there, which brought on a fit of giggles."

"It's a shame Jody can't go."

"I wouldn't let my kid go that far without me, either."

"I know." She moaned as his arms went around her waist and he pulled her against him.

The past year had been a whirlwind of happiness and love, more than she had ever dreamed of. There was no more guilt. No more bad feelings about the past. No more angst. Just life with a man she loved and a daughter she adored. She had the whole package, and never again would she let doubts and insecurities take over her life.

They'd gotten married in the small Catholic church, and her mother had been ecstatic because Angie had let her plan the wedding. Angie had picked out her dress and

Erin's. Doris had had the time of her life handling the rest. It had been stress-free for Angie and a happy occasion, even peaceful, which was a new standard for the Wiznowski family. The reception had been at the ranch, and then she and Hardy had flown away for a few days in the Bahamas.

Hardy kissed the hollow of her neck. She turned to him. She would never get tired of looking at his handsome face and the tall, lean body she could touch whenever she wanted. Now, that was heaven.

"Ready?" he asked. "We're leaving in fifteen minutes."

"Yes, sir." She saluted playfully and caught sight of herself in the full-length mirror. She stepped toward it. "Am I gaining weight? I bought these capris two weeks ago for the trip and they feel tight."

"You look the same—beautiful. But there could be another reason your pants feel tight."

She frowned. "What? Too much ice cream?"

He shook his head. "Have you thought you might be pregnant?"

"No...we've used protection."

"There were a couple of times I remember that we weren't too careful."

She looked in the mirror, with her hand on her stomach, and then her eyes caught his. "How would you feel about that?"

"Happy. Ecstatic." He smiled at her.

"Our lives would change," she mumbled almost to herself as the thought took root.

"Our lives are about to change anyway, so we might as well make it a full-meal deal. Are you ready for that?"

She met his gaze. "As long as you're with me."

"Always, beautiful."

She leaned into him, her heart full. "I'll buy a pregnancy test when we get back from our vacation, if I can wait that long." The excitement was already running through her system. Another child. That would be the icing on the cake of their happiness.

"In two weeks we'll be moving to the ranch," Hardy said. "My dad will be in and out of our lives when we do, but he has a room at his private club and he spends a lot of nights there."

She kissed his clean-shaven cheek. "Please stop worrying."

"I just want you and Erin to be happy."

"We are. Erin already loves the ranch and I feel confident we can make it work, especially since Mavis is retiring to spend more time with her grandchildren. But she's agreed to help out if we need her." She touched her stomach. "And we might. But we'll have the house to ourselves and the bakery is only eleven minutes from the ranch. No big deal. Except…"

"What?"

"The judge will probably continue to pressure you to run for office."

He gathered her into his arms. "He knows I'm not running unless I want to, and at the moment all I want is to spend time with my family. In another year, I might change my mind. But my wife will have a big say in that decision."

"Your wife will love and support whatever you want to do."

"Mmm. I don't want us living in a fishbowl with family around all the time. Though I do love them, I want time alone with you and Erin."

She poked him in the ribs. "Like that's going to happen being a member of the Wiznowski family."

He laughed. She loved it when he did that, and he was doing it more often these days. "I'm taking sweet Angie Wiznowski home with me for good."

"Oh, honey. She's been home with you for a while now."

"And I'm so grateful she finally agreed to love me forever." He took her lips in a hot, passionate kiss and they lost track of where they were for a brief moment. "We might have to buy a pregnancy test on the way to the airport. I can't wait, either."

"Mama, do you have my Cinderella sunglasses?" Erin called.

They slowly drew apart.

"Why would I have your sunglasses?"

"Because I can't find them."

"Did you look on the top of your head? That's where they were the last time you lost them."

A chuckle followed. "Yep. That's where they were. I want to take them with me. Aunt Patsy and Aunt Peggy gave them to me and they're funky. Oh, yeah. I'm funky."

"Ten minutes and everyone has to be in the car ready to go. Got it?"

"Got it, Dad!" Erin shouted back.

They were finally going to Disney World—as a family. They were flying out of Austin instead of driving. It had been a year of drama and changes, and they were all stronger for them. Even Erin. They'd been through a great deal and had come through everything with smiling faces and stronger spirits. Angie felt truly blessed. No longer would a secret weigh her down with guilt and indecisions. Love had filled her with confidence.

Hardy kissed her again and lifted her suitcase from the bed. "That means you, too, Mrs. Hollister."

She patted him on the butt as he walked out. In minutes she and Erin were in the kitchen, ready to leave on a vacation they'd dreamed about for years.

For a moment Angie looked around her home and knew life would be different when they returned. They would put the house on the market and move to the ranch. But she knew it would be a change for the better. They had a year of getting to know each other and growing as a family. Now they would go forward and make life even better. She just wished Rachel would come home.

Hardy was trying to get them out the door so they wouldn't mess up his time schedule.

Erin paused in the doorway with a hand on her pull suitcase. "I have something to say."

"Should I call the newspaper?"

"Daddy, I'm serious." Erin stomped her foot.

"Okay, what do you have to say?"

"I'm real happy we're a family now. Real happy. I didn't turn out weird or anything because of what happened. Everything's good."

Angie had to restrain herself from laughing out loud. Hardy had a difficult time, too.

Hardy recovered first. "Well, peanut, your mother and I are happy we're a real family, too. And we're extremely grateful you're not weird or anything."

Erin slipped the hot-pink feathery rhinestone sunglasses over her eyes. "Cool." Reaching into the sparkly purse Jody had given her for her birthday, she pulled out a tiara and placed it on her head. "While we're in Florida, I'd appreciate it if you'd call me Princess Erin from the House of Hollister."

Hardy looked at Angie. "What do you think?"

"Mmm...I suppose."

"Mama rules." Erin giggled and tugged her suitcase toward the door. "I have to text Jody that we're leaving."

"Remember, we talked about the constant texting," Angie reminded her.

Erin rolled her eyes and continued her journey to the car.

Hardy wrapped his arms around Angie. "We'd better have another child as fast as we can so we can stop spoiling this one."

"Too late," she whispered and stood on tiptoes to kiss him. "I love you."

"I love you, our life and our not-weird kid. I've never been this happy."

Angie snuggled into Hardy's arms and gave thanks for a time that could have destroyed them, but love had held them together. As it always would.

* * * * *

COMING NEXT MONTH FROM

H HARLEQUIN®

American Romance®

Available June 3, 2014

#1501 HER COWBOY HERO
The Colorado Cades
by Tanya Michaels

When Colin Cade gets a job on Hannah Shaw's ranch, he doesn't expect her to be so young and beautiful—or to have a little boy who reminds Colin of the one he lost.

#1502 THE TEXAN'S BABY
Texas Rodeo Barons
by Donna Alward

In the first book of a new six-book miniseries, Lizzie Baron feels the need to let loose—and she gets help from Christopher Miller, a sexy saddle bronc rider. But their night together leads to an unexpected result!

#1503 THE SEAL'S BABY
Operation: Family
by Laura Marie Altom

Libby Dewitt, pregnant and alone, brings out the hero in Navy SEAL Heath Stone. But can Libby help him overcome his tragic past and love again?

#1504 A RANCHER'S HONOR
Prosperity, Montana
by Ann Roth

It was only supposed to be one night of fun—after all, day care owner Lana Carpenter and rancher Sly Pettit have nothing in common. Until they discover a connection between them they never could have imagined...

HARCNM0514